SIGN OF THE CROSS

Shadow of the Rock

SIGN OF THE CROSS

THOMAS MOGFORD

B L O O M S B U R Y

LONDON • NEW DELHI • NEW YORK • SYDNEY

First published in Great Britain 2013

Map by ML Design

The moral right of the author has been asserted

Bloomsbury Publishing Plc
50 Bedford Square
London WC1B 3DP

www.bloomsbury.com

Bloomsbury Publishing, London, New Delhi, New York and Sydney

A CIP catalogue record for this book is available from the British Library

ISBN 978 1 4088 2918 9

10 9 8 7 6 5 4 3 2 1

Typeset by Hewer Text UK Ltd, Edinburgh
Printed and bound in Great Britain by CPI Group (UK) Ltd, Croydon CR0 4YY

for Jack and Molly

For beauty is but the beginning of terror.
We can barely endure it
and are awed
when it declines to destroy us.
Every angel is terrifying

Rilke, *Duino Elegies*

The woman's eyes are raised heavenwards. Her arms hang by her sides; her dress is pulled down to her waist. Deltas of blood criss-cross her pale stomach. Two neat, flat circles on her chest reveal where the breasts have been sliced from her body.

'David?'

Mifsud pulls his gaze away from the statue. The dark, empty streets of Valletta stretch ahead. 'Sorry, my love. You were saying?'

'Just that I've reached the point when I've –'

'Had enough,' Mifsud completes, taking his wife's hand, which slots neatly into his.

Teresa Mifsud's high heels echo on the flagstones. Her once black hair is a silvery grey. For years she dyed it, but now Mifsud has grown accustomed to its natural colour. Tonight she wears it tied into a chignon, revealing almost Slavic cheekbones and dark, thoughtful eyes.

Mifsud stops, cups a hand behind his wife's head and leans in to kiss her. The vintage claret from dinner is still seeping through his veins.

'What's got into you tonight?' Teresa asks, face brightening for the first time that evening.

'It'll be all right; trust me.' Mifsud smiles, then glances back at the statue, his eyes drawn by the marble halo carved around St Agatha's head. Teresa gently pulls him on. The street lamps create distant pools of yellow in the darkness.

'The Baron was in his element tonight,' Teresa says.

'All part of his ceremonial duties.'

'I think he was showing off to you. He was staring at us as we left.'

The proximity of Freedom Square to the bus terminus yields up the usual group of stragglers. Mifsud releases Teresa's hand, and she walks towards a tall, elegant woman in brown robes and a headscarf. The woman holds a baby strapped to her front in a sarong. Teresa leans in to kiss her hello, then steps back to peer at the baby's face. 'What's his name?'

'Saif.'

'David,' Teresa calls over, 'this is Dinah. And this sleepy little angel is Saif.'

The woman bows her long neck at Mifsud, who nods back. He hears a discreet 'tut' as a smartly dressed Maltese couple hurry by.

'David?'

Mifsud looks round. 'Goodbye, mister,' the woman calls out.

'One of yours?' Mifsud asks as they walk away.

'Used to be. They're moving her to the family camp now she's had the baby.'

'Libyan?'

'Somali.'

The city starts to empty out again on the other side of the piazza. They pass the shell of the Valletta Royal Opera House, bombed by the Luftwaffe, still not rebuilt. Mifsud finds Teresa's hand again, and she returns the pressure.

Turning onto Triq Sant'Orsla, Mifsud sees the windows of the Baron's palazzo still dark. They walk beneath his covered, overhanging balcony, then stop outside their own front door. The three locks are a legacy of the Baron's overcautious forebears: this flat once served as staff quarters. Mifsud follows his wife inside, then deadbolts the door behind them.

*　　*　　*

2

Placing the keys in the dish on the hallway table, Mifsud imagines Teresa next door, freeing her hair, pulling the sleek satin of her dress over her head. 'Nightcap, darling?' he calls through.

'Yes, please,' he hears as the shower starts to drip.

His features reflect back from the oval-shaped mirror above the mantelpiece, the tanned skin rendered darker now by the salt-and-pepper of his beard. Beneath his hooked nose – a touch of the Ottoman pirate, as Teresa likes to say – his lips twitch up at the corners. He is smiling; he cannot help it. He moves into the sitting room, passing the collection of baroque oils without a glance before entering the kitchen.

Lemon in the fridge, rum in the cupboard; spectacles on, Mifsud draws a carving knife from the block, running the blade up and down the metal sharpener, then clipping off the warty nubs of the lemon and quartering one half. The remaining half he wraps in cling film, replacing it in the fridge, wondering if they will retain these parsimonious habits once everything has changed. Probably not, he thinks, smile broadening further.

The kettle clicks off, steam curling from its spout. Mifsud takes out two china mugs, one decorated with a monkey and a 'Gibraltar Rocks!' logo, a long-ago present from his late sister. He spoons a measure of brown sugar into each, then follows up with a gener-ous slosh of rum. Checking the shower is still flowing, he raises the bottle to his lips, reasoning that they are celebrating, in a sense. A creaking comes from behind: just their ancient boiler, straining away. Humming to himself, Mifsud hammers the stop-per back in the bottle, then hears the noise again. He turns his head. A man is crouching by the side of the kitchen table. Mifsud stops humming.

The man straightens up, takes three paces across the floor and picks up the carving knife. From the bathroom, the dripping of the shower falls silent.

Mifsud closes his eyes. This is not possible, he thinks. How did he get in? When Mifsud opens his eyes, the man is holding a fingertip to his lips. Over his hands he wears white surgical gloves.

Teresa lets out a scream as she appears in the doorway. Her turban towel unravels in slow motion. Her hair is dark with water, comb grooves still visible.

Mifsud stands with his back to the kitchen wall. Through misted spectacles he watches as the man beckons to Teresa with the knife. She turns to Mifsud; he nods, and she crosses the floor, tightening the belt of her blue towelling dressing gown as she moves.

The intruder stares at her appraisingly. He wears an oil-stained white T-shirt, blue canvas trousers and flip-flops. A pink, incongruously feminine mouth sits in a powerful jaw. He points the tip of the knife at Teresa's abdomen. 'The cord,' he whispers, with a lingering roll of the 'r'.

Teresa glares at the man with such contempt that Mifsud wonders for a moment if they have met before. Even now, he thinks, the woman cannot hold her temper. Slowly she draws the cord from its eyes, then thrusts it towards him.

Folding the material over the blade, the man flicks upward. 'You,' he says to Mifsud. 'Arms out.'

Mifsud's hands hang protectively by his groin. He raises them up, aware of his tired old heart thumping as the soft towelling nooses his wrists.

'Sit down. Feet in front.'

Mifsud slides slowly down the wall, pushing out his legs as the man crouches before him, black brogues still beautifully polished for dinner. As the man binds his ankles, Mifsud wonders if he should kick out – Teresa could grab the knife, they might . . .

'Please,' Teresa whispers. 'We have jewellery. A little money . . .' She flinches as the man springs to his feet. In one swift, fluid motion, he draws his T-shirt up over his head. The muscles on his stomach are grotesquely defined, reminding Mifsud of Renaissance crucifixion scenes. Where was that altarpiece they saw in Sicily last year? Agrigento?

Mifsud snaps back to attention: the man is slicing his T-shirt in two. A wishbone of muscle contracts on each flank as he works the knife. 'Over there,' he says to Teresa. 'More to the side. Stretch across. Further . . .'

Teresa leans over the kitchen table, and the man squats by her head, using a strip of T-shirt to tie her wrists to the table leg. He has a tattoo on his back, Mifsud sees, rippling from his shoulder blades to the base of his spine. A black, eight-pointed Maltese cross.

The man swivels to Mifsud. 'Where is it?'

Mifsud catches a herbal reek on the man's breath. He glances at Teresa, who is lying with her cheek on her outstretched arms. She stares back, a soft arc of pale breast visible within the opening of her dressing gown.

'Where's the painting?' the man says.

'Painting?' Mifsud echoes. 'Take all of them, anything at all . . .' He is speaking quickly, voice nasal and flat.

The man raises the knife to Mifsud's neck. 'The valuable one.'

For the first time Mifsud hears uncertainty in the man's voice. The cool metal chills his throat. 'Next door,' he gasps. 'Above the desk.'

Lowering the blade, the man reaches for Mifsud's foot and yanks it upwards, wedging it between his bound wrists. Then he steps bare-chested into the sitting room.

Slumped on one side, Mifsud stares up at his wife. 'I love you,' she mouths, lips doing their best to smile. On the countertop above, steam still rises from the kettle. Mifsud tries to reach towards the knife block but his ankle is jammed between his wrists. Sweat blurs his eyes; he uses his forearm to feel in his trousers for his phone. His fingers are free; he manoeuvres them to his pocket . . .

'*David*,' Teresa hisses, and Mifsud looks round again. She shakes her head, and he nods back, spectacles slipping down his nose.

The next sound Mifsud hears is the rapid click-clack of flip-flops on the terracotta floor. Something in their rhythm quickens his heart still further. There is a clang as the knife is slammed down on the draining board. Picking up the bottle of rum, the man rears above. For a moment Mifsud thinks he is going to drink, but then he brings the bottle crashing down on the crown of Mifsud's head.

A wailing reverberates in Mifsud's ears. Wetness embraces his scalp. Somewhere Teresa is screaming. Surely the Baron or his wife will hear? Call the police? Then Mifsud remembers they are still at the dinner.

Stains float like clouds across his retinas. He opens his eyes and sees the jagged stump of the bottle lying on the floor beside him.

He looks up: the other half of the man's T-shirt has been stuffed into Teresa's mouth, the tails of her dressing gown flipped to the small of her back. Seeing the familiar, dimpled buttocks, he feels a heavy wave of sadness.

The man moves behind her, unzipping his flies. The high-pitched slapping makes Teresa scream again, muffled through her gag.

Mifsud tries to sit but his foot is still trapped. Flopping onto his back, he feels his scalp burn: shards of the bottle embedded in the skin.

He gazes round. His spectacles are spattered with blood but he can see that the man's thin brown penis has swollen, probing outwards, able to support its own weight. The man turns back to Mifsud. 'Last chance.'

'The Madonna and Child,' Mifsud says. 'Above the desk.'

'Not the Madonna. The Saint.'

Mifsud wants to be overwhelmed by fear, to be too disorientated to speak. But the clarity is there. Lurking beneath the surface is the clarity. 'I don't understand . . .' he groans.

Dipping into his pocket, the man draws out a silver, perforated square. He rips open the foil with his teeth, then replaces the wrapper in his pocket, rolling on the condom with a single, practised hand. Teresa struggles again with her bindings as the man reaches forward to her buttocks, parting them roughly. '*Haqq Alla!*' he curses in Maltese.

Teresa has swung a heel back into the man's shin. Picking up the knife, he leans forward and grabs her damp hair. She raises her chin defiantly as he holds the blade beneath her neck. 'Just try that again.'

Mifsud watches as the man plunges himself between Teresa's buttocks. The ringing in his ears grows louder. Teresa turns, one hand still clutching closed her dressing gown. The pointless attempt at modesty makes Mifsud catch his breath. 'Stop.'

The man pauses mid-thrust. Mifsud closes his eyes, waiting for the words to form, for the confession to come. A moment later, the thrusting resumes.

When Mifsud reopens his eyes, Teresa's expression has changed. All their life together she has known when he is lying. She knows it now.

Still staring down, she starts to shake her head. As she shakes it more vigorously, the blade of the knife licks against the tautened underside of her neck. Mifsud watches in puzzlement as a small purple bubble forms beneath the skin. Teresa peers down as well, then a moment later, a great arc of blood bursts outwards to the kitchen wall.

The man leaps back, dropping the knife. '*Fuck,*' he spits as the blood flows in rhythmic spurts from Teresa's neck. He zips up his flies as a final gout slaps onto the floor. Teresa's eyes start to glaze, but still she stares down at Mifsud, pupils boring into him.

The knife is just a yard away. Drawing his knees to his chest, Mifsud twists his foot from between his arms, feeling long-unused muscles rip across his back. Rotating on one hip, he puts his soles to the kitchen wall and pushes off like a swimmer turning. The smooth material of his dinner jacket slides easily over the tiled floor. Stretching out his fingers, he gets hold of the knife, then rolls onto his back.

Mifsud stares up at the ceiling, the flecks of glass in his skull making his head throb. Using both hands, he slides the tip of the knife down the buttons of his dress shirt, stopping when it finds the soft give of his belly.

The man appears above. Mifsud draws in a breath, then rams the knife with all his strength beneath his own ribcage. A strange, involuntary burping rises from his gullet. It feels as though he has been winded, a burning prickly heat creeping up his spine. When he can push no further, he pauses, then thrusts again. Something gives, and the knife seems to slide in more deeply. He tastes a sour, viscous fluid climbing his throat, senses the colour draining from his cheeks. Another jolt, then a gentle throbbing emptiness. When he closes his eyes, he thinks he sees Teresa's features, painted in chiaroscuro, blending with those of St Agatha as they dip in and out of vision.

The man is busy above, undoing Teresa's bindings, pressing the neck of the bottle into her hanging, lifeless hands. Mifsud senses his own bindings released, then the clip-clop of feet crossing the room. How can the man be leaving the flat half dressed? he wonders.

A smack, heard rather than felt, as Mifsud widens his eyes. It seems as though he is staring up through a muslin shroud.

'All your family,' he hears above. 'One by one unless you tell me now.'

Mifsud feels himself slipping towards unconsciousness.

'Where is it? *Where?*'

Mifsud breathes in. The movement racks his chest so much that he knows he will not repeat the motion. As he exhales for the last time, a single word passes his lips.

Then nothing.

PART ONE

Gibraltar

Chapter One

I

Spike Sanguinetti watched as the stipendiary magistrate slid on his spectacles and frowned at the document. It was not a good sign. Above the magistrate's bald head, the lion and the unicorn continued their tussle for the royal coat of arms. 'And where are the co-defendants in this matter?' he asked.

'It is our understanding that the DNA evidence relating to the co-defendants has still not been processed,' Spike replied. 'Given that my client has already been on remand for over three months, we moved to hold the hearing at the first available opportunity.'

'And what is the Crown's position on this?'

Spike glanced over at Drew Stanford-Trench, who was still shuffling through his court bundle, handsome face pale and blotchy. In the afternoon light slanting through the courtroom's high windows, Spike saw fine blond hairs growing from his ear like mould. 'The prosecution would simply reiterate the reasons for remand in the first place,' Stanford-Trench said. 'Until the owner of the yacht has been traced, the defendant cannot safely be given bail.'

'Safely?'

'Reasonably.' A drip of alcoholic sweat fell from Stanford-Trench's nose, forming a damp corona on the top sheet of his papers. Winter hours in court: air conditioning not yet on.

'Your Worship,' Spike said, taking over, 'in view of the length of time that has passed since the preliminary hearing, might it not be sensible to sum up the agreed facts of the case?'

The magistrate took off his spectacles and sat back; Stanford-Trench shot Spike a grateful glance.

Spike continued. 'On 6 November last year, the defendant, Mr Harrington, registered with an online company seeking volunteers to crew a yacht between the Caribbean and Montenegro. Having been allocated the position of first mate on *The Restless Wave*, Mr Harrington flew to St Martin in the expectation of an enjoyable holiday during which he might improve his sailing skills. He had not met the other crew members; they had not met each other. The yacht was subjected to a routine search on departure from St Martin; on bunkering in Gibraltar, however, a sniffer dog alerted our customs officers, who uncovered a small fibreglass compartment hidden in the hold. Inside lay eighteen slabs of uncut cocaine. My client has always denied any knowledge of the drugs, and feels, not to put too fine a point on it, that he and the other crew members have been set up.'

Spike looked over at the dock. Three months in Her Majesty's Prison, Gibraltar, had done a good job of bleeding out the rich yachtsman's tan with which Piers Harrington had arrived on the Rock. His hair remained sun-bleached only at the tips, which now spilled over his ears. His long grey face stared ahead, hollow-eyed.

'No connection,' Spike went on, looking back at the magistrate, 'has ever been found between Mr Harrington and the owner of the yacht, a man about whom little is known other than the fact that he is a Serbian national. My client's lengthy stay in prison has apparently been necessitated by the painstaking work performed by forensics in London, who have sought to determine if Mr Harrington's DNA could be connected to the drugs or the secret compartment. As Your Worship can now see from the report, no such DNA link has been established. We request, therefore, not that Mr Harrington be granted bail, but that all charges against him be dropped.'

'Mr Stanford-Trench?' the magistrate said. 'Are you in a position to join us now?'

'Absolutely, Your Worship. It has recently emerged that the yacht owner, a Mr . . .' Stanford-Trench peered down – 'Radovic, purchased *The Restless Wave* through a shell company incorporated here in Gibraltar. Though Interpol are yet to trace his whereabouts, the paper trail is starting to hot up and –'

'Starting to hot up?' the magistrate interrupted. 'You've had ninety days to penetrate this mystery while Mr Harrington has been languishing in prison.'

'Your Worship,' Stanford-Trench said, 'I respectfully submit that a colleague had charge of the case at that time, and as she is now on maternity leave, it has fallen to me to –'

'Enough, Mr Stanford-Trench. Sit down.' The magistrate turned to the dock. 'Mr Harrington?'

Spike looked over at his client, making an upwards motion with his fingers. Harrington blinked his sunken eyes and stood.

'Mr Harrington,' the magistrate resumed, 'I regret that you have been held without bail for so long, but the trafficking of twenty-two kilograms of cocaine is a very serious offence. I understand that you have recently retired to Sotogrande after a long and unblemished career in the City of London. What was supposed to be the start of an exciting new chapter of your life has therefore turned into something of a nightmare. The court of Gibraltar hereby drops all charges against you. The prosecution will no doubt reserve the right to revert to you at a later date for further questioning, but for now you are free to go.'

Piers Harrington turned to Spike, who smiled back, gesturing at the door. Finally understanding, Harrington bowed at the magistrate, then exited with his custody officer.

The clerk began calling out details from the next docket. Alongside him on the bench, Spike heard Drew Stanford-Trench give a long, slow sigh as he packed away his papers.

2

'Cheer up,' Peter Galliano said. 'It's another win.'

'On the facts.'

'But you're going great guns. Top earner this month at Galliano & Sanguinetti.'

Given that there were just two of them at the firm, this was no accolade.

'And a mere thirty-five years old –'

'Thirty-six,' Spike corrected.

Galliano raised a pudgy hand to attract the attention of the waitress. They sat together at the head of a trestle table outside the All's Well in Casemates Square, a pub named in honour of the refrain used by British soldiers at night to confirm that the gates of Gibraltar were safe. The Rock loomed above, its bone-white lime-stone lit up for the non-existent winter tourist. The fresh poniente wind was dropping, but it was still mid-teens, icy for Gibraltarians. As Spike flipped up the collar of his overcoat, he remembered an Italian phrase of his father's – '*Febbraio, febbraietto, corto e male-detto*', 'February, little February, short and cursed'. Yes, he thought as he finished his pint, that was about the size of it.

Midway down the table, Jessica Navarro was crouching to talk to another guest. She wore a grey pencil skirt and tight ribbed jumper. Catching Spike's eye over the shoulder of her companion, she threw him a smile.

'*Vale*,' Galliano said, signalling to the waitress. 'How many are we, Spike? Fifteen?'

'Twenty-two.'

Galliano puffed out his cheeks. '*Waka* . . . Twenty-two shots of sambuca.'

The waitress jotted the number down.

'And lots of crisps,' Galliano called after as she returned to the bar.

On the other side of the table, a tall blond man in a blazer and cashmere roll-neck was expertly working the guests. Spike watched him reward a comment with a raised hand, which became a high five.

'M'learned friends?'

Spike stood to his full height, then leaned down to kiss Jessica hello, catching a scent he didn't recognise. Still seated, Galliano reached up to draw her hand into his suspiciously black goatee. 'Get 'em in while I can,' he said, smothering her fingers with kisses.

As Jessica started to crouch, Spike pulled across a plastic chair. 'Please. You're making me feel unfit.'

She smiled, then positioned the chair facing both of them. Her chestnut hair looked as though it had been freshly cut. As she tossed it over one shoulder, Spike caught a crimson flash of bra strap.

'*Muncho chachi*,' he said, slipping into *yanito*, the patois used by native Gibraltarians.

'What, this old thing?' Jessica replied, arching an eyebrow.

'May I?' Spike indicated her left hand, and they both leaned in to admire the chunky octagonal diamond on its thin platinum band. Spike thought of his mother's engagement ring, buried somewhere in the chaos of Rufus's bedroom. About a tenth of the size, a cluster of yellow diamonds in a daisy setting. 'The biggest rock on the Rock,' he said. 'So . . . up for a late one?'

Jessica shook her head. 'Hamish has to fly to Switzerland tomorrow morning.'

'All OK?'

'Just a few meetings . . . Speak of the devil.'

Hamish Ferguson appeared alongside Spike. His well-tamed blond curls gave him the air of a young Roman warrior heading out for battle. The proud disdainful face left little doubt as to the probable result of the campaign. 'Heard a heck of a lot about you,' he said, crisp English accent bearing no trace of his alleged Glaswegian roots.

17

'Congratulations.'

The handshake was delivered with a well-honed burst of pain. 'When you know, you know.'

'You remember Peter Galliano?' Jessica said.

Galliano smoothed down his goatee with a hand. 'You're a hedgie, right?'

'For my sins.'

'Grab a pew and I'll tell you why your fund's with the wrong law firm.'

'Peter . . .' Spike said.

'No, it's OK,' Hamish replied, touching Spike's shoulder benevolently. He glanced – almost imperceptibly – at his Rolex then sat down beside Galliano.

Spike retook his seat. He was used to seeing Jessica in police uniform. Tonight she wore lipstick, smoky eyeliner; he thought he had never seen her look so beautiful. 'It's just such great –'

'OK, Spike, you've done your bit.' She moved her chair closer. 'Another victory, they tell me.'

'A monkey would have won.'

'That's not what I heard.'

'I didn't think newly promoted detectives paid attention to small fry in the magistrates' court.'

The waitress interrupted with a tray of shots. 'Whoa!' Hamish boomed, eyeing his colleagues at the end of the table.

'They come with one proviso,' Galliano said. 'That you let me take you out to lunch to explain what Galliano & Sanguinetti can do for you and your team at Charon Partners.'

'What? Oh, right. Sure.' Grabbing eight shots in his large hands, Hamish set off up the table. Jessica smiled over at Galliano – 'You shouldn't have'– then stood to help the waitress distribute the rest.

'Arsehole,' Galliano muttered. He kept his eyes on Jessica as she laughed with another guest. 'Apparently he's being head-hunted for some fund in Zug.'

'Will he take the job?'

'You mean, will she follow?' Galliano held Spike's eye, then mock-slapped his own forehead. '*Bezims*,' he cursed. 'The crisps.' He began the slow process of shunting his chair backwards.

'I'll go,' Spike said, standing.

3

The other tables outside the All's Well were empty, punters driven away either by the engagement party, or by the fact that it was a Tuesday night in February. Inside, even the karaoke machine was off. A few solitary drinkers sat cradling pints of bitter.

The waitress was smoking behind the bar. 'Three packs of salt and vinegar,' Spike said.

'Sorry. The box is down in the storeroom.'

'*Harampai*,' Spike replied, 'finish your cigarette first.' He turned and scanned the muted sports channel on the pub TV. Some kind of junior tennis tournament – players looked about twelve. His ear was caught by a curious, softly spoken accent. Alone at a corner table, a figure sat hunched over a mobile phone.

Spike moved closer. The man was listening intently; a moment later he launched into a fluent reply, speaking in a strange Slavonic language, vowels issuing from the back of his throat.

Moving to one side, Spike made out the sweaty face of Piers Harrington. His sun-bleached hair had been tidied up at the barber's. His eyes shone hard and uneasy in his gaunt face.

Spike turned back to the bar, where the waitress stubbed out her cigarette and rose to her feet. 'Change of plan,' he said. 'A glass of champagne for the man in the corner.'

The waitress peered around Spike's shoulder; Harrington was still talking, the bony fingers of one hand clasped over his head, like a spider feeding off his skull.

'Tell him Spike Sanguinetti is impressed by his command of Serbian.'

'Impressed by his command of Serbian,' the waitress repeated uncertainly.

He gave her a twenty-pound note. 'That's too much,' she called after, but he was already out on the terrace.

Hamish Ferguson's booming laugh cut through the February air. On the other side of Casemates, the unsteady figure of Drew Stanford-Trench was shepherding two girls through the entrance to the Tunnel nightclub. Spike turned away and walked in the direction of the Old Town.

4

The shops on Main Street were locked up for the night. Spike stared through the security grilles at the tawdry, duty-free displays. This city: once a proud impenetrable fortress, now cravenly begging for custom. A green cleaning truck was inching down the cobbles, flanked by two boiler-suited Moroccans furiously hosing down the gutters. Spike felt a fine salty mist on his face as he passed.

Defend your client, Galliano liked to say. Defend your client and let the law take care of itself.

Spike wiped his forehead and continued towards John Mackintosh Square, where Old Man Gaggero was on his nightly walk, fag in one hand, blue bag of excrement in the other, waiting as his dog marked its territory in fitful spurts over the parliament building. He gave Spike his usual wave; Spike nodded back, then turned up the steps to the Old Town.

The familiar maze of ramps and alleyways unwound before him. As he came into Chicardo's Passage, he took out his keys, seeing the same cracked *azulejos* around the lintel, the same window boxes of dying oleanders – a horticultural hospice surviving purely on his father's palliative applications of Baby Bio.

Inside, General Ironside raised his head from his basket. His grey muzzle bobbed, as though he couldn't quite fathom why his joints wouldn't spring him to his feet. Spike crouched down, stroking the wiry hair behind his ears. The General's stumpy Jack Russell tail managed a wag before his head began to droop again.

In the kitchen, Rufus's watercolour set still lay on the table, alongside the foil remnants of another M&S steak-and-kidney pudding. Spike swept the latter into the bin, then pushed through the bead curtain and up the creaking staircase.

He stooped his six-foot-three frame down to stare into the bathroom mirror, a constant since his schooldays, unlike the reflection within it. Two faint bracket lines were visible now between Spike's nose and mouth, like a warning that some time soon smiling would exist only in parentheses. He pushed back his dark hair. At least his eyes were unchanged: bright blue irises in a tanned, angular face. Such kind eyes, people always said. Blue eyes in a Scandinavian were chilly; worn by a dark-skinned Gibraltarian and a warm heart was the assumption.

Stretching out on his childhood bed, his mind drifted back to the events of last year. Once again, he'd ignored the basic lesson. Trust no one. However innocent, however needy. No one.

His phone was vibrating. He picked it up from the bedside table, anticipating Jessica's name on the screen. Number withheld. 'Yes?'

'Spike?'

The familiar, husky tones made Spike sit up.

'I wasn't sure if I should call,' said Zahra.

'Are you OK?'

'As well as can be expected. How are *you*?'

'You know. Another day in paradise. Why do you ask?'

'I just wanted to say . . . I'm sorry.'

'Sorry for what?'

Zahra paused. 'You mean you haven't heard?'

'Heard what?'

'*Naik*,' Zahra cursed in Arabic, and it was then that Spike knew something had happened to his uncle and aunt.

✳

The woman stands on the concrete dock, staring out at the marina. Boats creak in the breeze; in the starlight, she makes out the strange eyes painted on their flanks, winking as they dip in and out of the oily water.

She wonders which boat will be hers. Moored on the furthest jetty is a trawler, more stable than the wooden skiff which brought her here to Malta, which they had to bail out using plastic tubs. Yes . . . she hopes it will be that one.

She checks the pocket of her robes for the rolled-up notes. She feels guilty about not telling her friends, but there was only one place left on the boat, and she needs to get away from the Idiot, from the one who was too selfish to put Saif before himself. The woman smiles at the thought of him still stuck here in the camp. She will text her friends soon enough. Maybe she will find a way for them to follow her over the water.

The movement wakes Saif. The woman eases out her left breast and feels the familiar tingle as he latches firmly on.

Above her the stars pulse in the sky. She remembers how bright they looked in the desert, each one a sun, the Idiot had told her as they lay together.

Saif gives a whimper. She knows him by now; loosening her sarong, she transfers him to her other breast, clasping his chubby backside with both hands. The rhythmic sucking resumes.

'My little boy,' she whispers, peering down. 'Bright star of my life.'

How quickly he grows – stealing the weight from her, her friends say. No matter, she will need to be lean for the work. Restaurants the size of marketplaces. She will have to fetch and carry, look after the customers, maybe one will catch her eye, the loveliest girl in Berbera, that's what they used to say.

Her shoulders start to ache, so she adjusts her grip. She thinks again of the footballer she saw on the TV. His skin darker than hers, but speaking Italian like a native son. She imagines Saif taking care of her, gently correcting her language with a confident smile, moving into a big house with a family of his own.

The boats creak in a fresh burst of breeze. A smell of faeces reaches her nose. The men's camp is just round the corner: typical of them to create such a stench. The moon seems higher in the sky. How long has she been here? she wonders. Is she in the right place? But the instructions were clear and she rarely makes mistakes when she has time to think things through.

She glances over her shoulder. The warehouses set into the wall behind have bars on the gates; inside, she makes out the fibreglass silhouettes of tigers' muzzles, dragons' snouts – models for the Carnival, the man had said. She is in the right place.

Though there is no one else on the dock, she still holds her breath to listen for movement. She thinks again of home, of how she used to wake at night before her brothers snuck back in – before they'd even parted the curtains she would be lying there, eyes closed, pretending not to hear as they clambered into bed, reeking of maize beer. She has that same premonition now, but perhaps it is just Saif, whose feeding always starts to slow as sleep begins to –

The woman's neck jerks back. She feels a muscular arm loop around her shoulders, pulling her backwards. She wants to lash out, but her hands are still supporting Saif. Drawing in a breath to scream, she feels something soft pressed against her mouth and nose.

Sweet antiseptic vapours seep through her nostrils. Her head begins to swim; as she gathers Saif closer, fatigue starts to overwhelm her. The stars turn to yellow streaks in the sky. When she breathes in again, her eyelids flicker.

Her muscles feel tired and heavy. A voice in her head says, Keep holding on, Keep your arms up, but she is powerless to obey as her body starts to relax. Her arms droop. The sharp clamp of gums on her breast wakes her just long enough to feel Saif rolling down her front, followed by the heavy, hollow thump of his head on the concrete.

PART TWO

Malta

Chapter Two

I

Spike checked the map, then walked left into Triq ir-Repubb-lika. He didn't know Valletta well – his last visit had been with his mother – but it was still hard to get lost in Europe's smallest capital. The Knights of St John had founded their city on an uninhabited limestone promontory, laying out the streets in a grid. The height of the buildings, and their rigid geometry, some-times put him in mind of a sixteenth-century precursor to Manhattan.

Dusk was falling, the people streaming for the exits. A quirk of Valletta: the capital of Malta, yet few locals actually lived here, drawn by the cheaper developments of Sliema and St Julian's. The older families still had their palazzos; otherwise, the permanent inhabitants of Valletta tended to be those who loved the baroque architecture too much to leave. Like his uncle and aunt, Spike thought grimly, a sinking feeling returning to his stomach.

Two attractive, dark-haired women in trouser suits strode ahead, each carrying pink-ribboned legal briefs: with its tax breaks and online gaming firms, Malta had almost as high a proportion of lawyers as Gibraltar.

At the end of the street rose the City Gate, a monumental arch signifying the outer limits of Valletta. Milling around its columns lounged half a dozen bored-looking black men. The odd Maltese waited alone, checking a watch, using the gate as an after-work meeting point. Spike searched for Maltese and Africans together but found none.

Passing beneath the central archway, Spike saw a plaque on the wall declaring Valletta's status as a UNESCO World Heritage Site. He emerged onto the walkway which ran across the St James Ditch, a vast, fifty-foot-deep moat built to protect Valletta's landward approach from intruders. The rest of Valletta was surrounded by sea walls: winch up this drawbridge and the city became an island within an island.

Ahead sprawled the bus terminus, a roundabout of concentric circles with a fountain in the middle, three bronze statues of Triton, son of Poseidon, holding up a spurting dish. Spike remembered Malta's buses as clapped-out Bedfords and Leylands, customised by their owner-drivers with grilles and slogans, their orange-and-yellow livery more suited to the 1960s Caribbean than to Europe. Now, a fleet of low-floored Arriva buses encircled the fountain, painted in cream and aquamarine, their EU-regulated, reduced-emission engines droning away.

Next came the Phoenicia Hotel, a luxury art-deco affair with verdant lawns and an eager team of porters opening a shiny car door for each arrival. The contrast with the two-star dive where Spike and his father were staying was marked: last-minute rooms in central Valletta had been hard to come by. Spike stopped, checking the tatty tourist map he'd picked up in reception. The street names were all in Maltese: 'triq' this, 'triq' that, the bizarre accents and clusters of 'x's, 'j's and 'q's rendering even a mental pronunciation impossible.

The suburb of Floriana felt more Gibraltarian in its loose masonry and discarded sun-bleached rubbish. Spike came into a square where two broad rectangular buildings faced off against each other. The first was of rusticated stone, a bas-relief of the madonna set above the pediment and a polished marble plaque revealing it as the Curia, the administrative headquarters of the Catholic Church. The second looked more functional: satellite dishes on the roof, walls topped with razor wire. The twin guardians of Maltese society, Spike thought to himself: Church and Police.

2

The fat duty sergeant almost filled the glass booth. His blue uniform looked British-inspired, but his face – already blackened by half a day's stubble – was pure southern Mediterranean. Spike imagined him gunning down rare songbirds in the summertime, then barking at his wife to roast them up.

'I'm here about the Mifsud case,' Spike said.

'I'll need some . . .' the sergeant began, but Spike was already sliding his British Gibraltar passport through the gap beneath his window.

Breathing heavily through his nose, the sergeant scrutinised Spike's photo, frowning as he tried to reconcile the easy smile of a few years back with the stern face of the man before him. Blu-tacked to his booth were various A4 mugshots of African men. A dog-eared poster offered instructions on how much of a drug called 'khat' was considered legal.

'Signature,' the sergeant grunted, returning the passport, then shoving a clipboard through the gap.

Once Spike had signed, the sergeant passed over an envelope containing heavy iron keys. 'Forensics finished already?' Spike asked as he examined their skeletal, old-fashioned shape.

The sergeant shrugged.

'Where I come from, a murder investigation isn't something we tie off in a week.'

'And where might that be?' came a voice.

Spike turned to see a young man in a well-cut, navy suit standing behind him. The man's slicked-back dark hair and finely boned features appeared too delicate for police work; he looked more like a catalogue model, or a heart-throb head boy ready for prize-giving.

'Gibraltar,' Spike said.

'Where they still do things the British way.'

'The thorough way.'

The young man turned, then punched a code into a keypad. 'You'd better come with me, Mr Sanguinetti,' he said, holding open a side door.

3

The corridor carpet was thin and frayed, the ceiling mosaicked with fungus. 'My PA said you'd be coming by . . . I thought you'd be younger, somehow,' the man called over his shoulder. 'You're the nephew, right?' His Maltese English had an Italianate bounce, more aggressive than Spike's gentle Hispanic lilt. The legacies of Empire ran to accents.

'Yes, but I'm here in a professional capacity.'

'Oh?'

'Executor of the wills.'

The man stopped and turned. He couldn't have been more than twenty-five, a full decade younger than Spike. 'Assistant Commissioner Mark Azzopardi,' he said, holding Spike's gaze. 'I had charge of the case.'

'Spike Sanguinetti.'

Azzopardi pumped Spike's hand, then ushered him through another door. Given the colonial scale of the main building, the squad room was surprisingly small, a dozen or so plain-clothed officers squeezed opposite one another at desks, computer monitors back to back. Azzopardi glanced at each as he passed; they responded with a polite nod.

The assistant commissioner's office was little more than a desk surrounded by filing cabinets. Evidently the Curia was winning the battle for Malta's taxes. The walls were crammed with diplomas: between Azzopardi's 'Firing Range Commendation' and 'Malta Police Academy Order of Merit' hung a cracked icon of the madonna.

'My condolences,' Azzopardi said as he sat. 'Now, how can I help?'

'I was just curious,' Spike said, folding himself into a chair opposite, 'to understand why you aren't still at the murder scene.' The back of the desk obliged him to contort his long legs to one side.

'The case is closed.'

'You don't think it's strange that a man with no history of violence would kill his wife then himself?'

Azzopardi uncrossed his arms. He wore a striped friendship bracelet on one wrist. 'Solicitor or barrister?' he said, as though offering Spike a choice between heads or tails.

'In Gibraltar the profession is fused.'

'Malta too. But do you do much criminal work?'

'Enough.'

Azzopardi reached into a drawer and pulled out a file. His hand hesitated. 'Mrs Mifsud . . . Teresa. I presume she's the blood relative?'

Spike shook his head. 'David was my mother's brother.'

An edge of reappraisal entered Azzopardi's gaze. 'But you were close?'

Trying to read Spike's expression, but failing, Azzopardi passed over the first photograph. David Mifsud lay on his back on the tiled kitchen floor. He wore black tie, his dinner jacket open, tails splayed behind. His hands were clasped across his stomach, like a knight on the lid of a tomb, Spike thought, dimpled knife hilt glinting between interlaced fingers. The entire blade was concealed beneath his ribcage. What had once been a white dress shirt was now rusty with blood.

31

'Mr Sanguinetti?' Azzopardi said.

Spike stared down at his uncle's bespectacled face. The grey tip of his tongue was visible, as though he were doing up his shoelace, or trying to change a light bulb. His expression of concentration reminded Spike so much of his mother that he had to lay the photograph on his lap to stop his hands shaking.

'They'd been out at a ceremonial dinner,' Azzopardi said, tipping his chair back and tucking his hands behind his head. 'Drunk a lot of wine. Your uncle topped up with rum when they got home.'

'Who called it in?'

'Neighbour said they weren't answering the door. The bodies had been there forty-eight hours by the time we arrived.'

'Suicide by stabbing . . . Seen much of that?'

Azzopardi said nothing.

'Why not just slit the wrists?'

'The forensic psychologist tells me a knife to the belly is a sign of the profoundest self-loathing. It does happen, apparently.'

Azzopardi tipped his chair forward, then handed Spike two more photographs. The first showed Teresa, slumped on her front on the kitchen table. Her grey hair pooled around her head; her cheek lay flat on the knotted wood between her arms. Decorating the wall behind her was an explosion of blood. There followed a close-up of her face, sagging neck encrusted with blood, eyes pearlescent, glaring down with what looked like hatred. A greenish tinge to the forehead gave a first hint of decomposition.

Spike formed the photographs into a pile and passed them back, hand now steady. 'My uncle was not capable of this.'

'His prints were the only ones on the knife.'

'Someone could have broken in. Dressed the scene.'

'A ground-floor apartment? The front door triple-bolted, the windows barred? In order to gain entry, my Mobile Squad had to take a hacksaw to the bedroom window . . .'

Spike looked over at the photographs on the desk. Teresa was missing her dressing-gown cord, he saw.

'The only other prints in the flat were your aunt's. They didn't even have domestic help.'

'Assuming for one moment it was murder–suicide – what's the motive?'

Azzopardi glanced down at his perfectly filed nails. 'There's an aspect of the case we've chosen to treat with delicacy.'

'Which is?'

'The pathologist who carried out the post-mortem on your aunt. He found traces of spermicide. The quantity suggested use of a condom.'

'So?'

'So in Malta, married couples don't tend to indulge much in contraception. Especially when they're of a certain age.' Azzopardi pressed on hurriedly. 'Forensic tests on your uncle showed no indications of recent sexual activity. No prophylactics of any kind were found in the flat . . .'

'So you're trying to tell me my aunt was having an affair?'

Azzopardi returned to the file, flicking through like an estate agent seeking particulars of the right property. Lighting upon one photograph, he passed it over. A broken bottle; next came an image of a towel discarded by the kitchen doorway. 'Your aunt's prints were all over the bottle of rum,' Azzopardi said, leaning back again in his chair. 'Your uncle downs half before confronting her. They struggle, the towel falls. She grabs the bottle and breaks it over his head. Then he really loses it. They're in the kitchen, he goes for a knife. An argument over adultery turns into a bloodbath. It's a common scenario, even in Malta. Just rarely with this much violence.' A note of relish had crept into Azzopardi's voice; Spike gave him back the photographs the wrong way up.

'Any DNA evidence from this third party?'

Azzopardi shook his head.

'Then why aren't you trying to track him down?'

Azzopardi glanced up at the icon of the madonna. 'As you may have noticed, Mr Sanguinetti, Malta remains an extremely Catholic country. Until recently, the Church wouldn't allow the burial of suicides on holy ground. Abortion is still banned, we've only just legalised divorce. Do you know the only two countries behind us in that regard? The Vatican and the Philippines.' He hazarded a sympathetic smile. 'You want the whole of Valletta society to know your aunt had a lover on the side? At times like this the police prefer . . . discretion.'

'Church and police in perfect harmony.'

'You got it,' Azzopardi said, apparently missing the ironic tone.

Spike put his palms to his cheeks, feeling the rasp of fresh stubble. When he looked back, a business card had appeared between Azzopardi's elegant fingers. 'Any questions, you can reach me here at the Depot.'

'The Depot?'

'Our local word for the police station.' He stood. 'Let me show you out.'

Spike declined, walking alone through the squad room back to the foyer, where the fat duty sergeant still sat at his booth, filling in forms.

Out in the square, Spike leaned against the side wall of the Curia, jaw clenched as he steadied his breathing. Then he turned back towards Valletta.

4

Just 6.10 p.m. and the city was deserted. A cool February breeze was gusting in off the Mediterranean up the deep, straight gullies of the streets. Spike could see why Jean de Valette, Grand Master of the Knights, had chosen a grid structure for his city: ventilation. He tugged down the sleeves of his navy V-neck and continued towards Triq Sant'Orsla.

A red British phone box stood guard on the street corner. The cobblestones fell away: Valletta's limestone promontory was kinked in the middle, weighed down by its residential cargo, like a beast of burden with a buckled spine. The pavements at the sides of the road were notched with steps.

At each cross street, Spike looked up at the omnipresent statuary: saints slaying dragons, madonnas cradling babies, Jesus lugging his cross. He found himself pining for the mildewed concrete of Gibraltar.

At last he saw the palazzo, dominating the entire corner of Triq it-Teatru l-Antiq – Old Theatre Street, presumably. After walking beneath its protruding, covered balcony, he stopped outside his uncle and aunt's front door.

A window further down was boarded up. As Spike manoeuvred the iron keys from his pocket, he caught a twitch of movement to the left. He looked up, but the windows of the palazzo were dark, the curtains still. The wind whistled through the empty street behind as he slotted the first key into the lock.

The smell of disinfectant hit him as soon as he opened the door. The decor looked unchanged since his last visit: Japanese paper shade in the hallway, dark-spotted mirror above the mantelpiece. Spike had yet to read the Mifsud wills but the beneficiaries were unlikely to be retiring to Monaco.

After gathering the utility bills from the mat – they would need to be settled by the estate – he headed into the kitchen. Everything seemed tidy: chairs tucked neatly against the table, blistered Le Creuset pots hanging from a rack, green and yellow sponges left on the work surface – accidental spoor of the industrial cleaner.

Gradually the photos Spike had seen at the Depot began to superimpose themselves on the room. He imagined drunken yells, Teresa attacking Mifsud with a bottle before he threw her onto the kitchen table and ran a knife across her gullet. The knife turned on himself . . . His Uncle David? *Really?*

The far wall was covered with a gloss of fresh paint. He checked for bloodstains on the terracotta tiles: nothing. Next door, a dated-looking ball gown had been laid out on the bed. Feeling a sudden sting of sadness, he moved to the sitting room.

The same collection of oils in their chipped giltwood frames, the same low, round table, fanned now with documents relating to the Mission of St John Hospitaller, the NGO his aunt had worked for: teaching aids, flyers requesting donations. On the desk sat a silver photo frame: David and Teresa on their honeymoon, he already middle-aged and bearded, she with jet-black hair and a toothy smile, standing proudly in front of a ruined temple as though they'd been the first to discover it.

A dampness came to Spike's eyes. He blinked it away, then reached for the desk drawer, feeling the tremor in his hands once again. Inside lay an address book and a pile of academic diaries. The top diary was for the current year; as he started to flick through, seeing the entries in his uncle's fine italic writing, he heard a knock. He waited, motionless, until the knock came again. Slipping the diary into his pocket, he turned out the lights and returned to the hallway.

5

There was no spyhole in the door, so Spike cautiously undid the latch, pushing the heavy oak frame outwards. Nothing but dark, empty street. He stuck his head out further. An old man was standing a few yards away on the cobbles.

The man's tailored blue shirt was tucked into pressed charcoal slacks. Filaments of faded blond hair were teased back over his head. A clipped, almost military moustache retained the darker shade the rest of his hair had lost. 'Is that . . . Spike?' he said.

Spike stared back.

'My good God, it is.' The man lowered a bulky mobile phone and slid it into the pocket of his trousers. 'I heard a noise downstairs,' he said in an educated, faintly European accent. 'I was about to call the police. It's Michael, Michael Malaspina. Don't you remember?'

'The Baron?'

The Baron smiled indulgently. 'Just Michael.' His eyes glinted with a youthful intensity, at odds with the liver-spotted brow. Close up, he was a good foot shorter than Spike. 'But won't you come in? No, you're not in the mood. I can see that.'

Spike motioned behind with a thumb. 'I'm doing an inventory. Itemising the contents of the flat.'

The Baron's moustache twitched in bemusement.

'As executor of the wills.'

'Of course,' the Baron said, 'you're the lawyer. David was so proud.' He lowered his gaze, lost for a moment in reminiscence. 'But won't you come for supper?' He raised his bright eyes. 'Tomorrow perhaps?'

'Tomorrow would be great. I'm here with my father . . .'

Spike thought he saw the Baron flinch. He was used to that when Rufus was mentioned.

'Even better,' the Baron recovered with a smile. 'It's been far too long.' He peered round Spike's shoulder to the open doorway, where the post was now piled on the hallway table. 'You're not staying *in* the flat, are you?'

'Hotel.'

'Quite right . . . Natalya will be thrilled. Eight for eight thirty?'

Once the Baron had shuffled round the corner to the main entrance of the palazzo, Spike turned back to the hallway. The musty, charity-shop smell began to nauseate him, but he forced himself back inside and continued his work.

6

It was past midnight when Spike returned to the hotel. The night porter was struggling with a sudoku puzzle in *The Times of Malta*. Spike asked him to check again if there were any single rooms, and received the same reply as on arrival: Carnival next week, the whole island fully booked.

He started up the stairs, his tiredness offset by the quiet satisfaction at having completed a task. The twin room he was sharing with his father was on the second floor; as he opened the door, he expected to see Rufus's scrawny frame enshrouded in the nearest bed. He flicked on the lights. The room was empty.

Turning back to the landing, he slammed the lift button, before abandoning it for the stairs. Three flights led up to the roof terrace; he shouldered open the fire door and scanned the flat, moonlit space. In the centre rose a covered dining area, already laid for breakfast, perspex windows providing a cloudy protection from the breeze. Around the outside, wooden tables were positioned to admire the view. At the furthest, silhouetted against the night sky, sat his father. Spike set off towards him.

Rufus was staring over the railings at the glittering tongue of the Grand Harbour below. The breeze fluffed out his white, shoulder-length hair. 'Oh,' he said. 'It's you.'

'Were you expecting someone else?'

He turned back to the railings. 'You can see the dockyard from up here. They were loading a ship.'

Spike placed a hand on his father's shoulder, feeling the shoulder blade jut beneath his cotton shirt, the bone as light as balsa wood. 'Come on, Dad. Let's get you back downstairs.'

His father remained seated, so Spike pulled up a chair. Beyond him spread the skyline of Valletta, its towers and cupolas alight, their ornate splendour an insult to the stolid practicality of Gibraltar.

'I've been thinking about your uncle David,' Rufus said.

'Me too.'

'He told me something once. That he would never take his own life. Under any circumstances.'

'Because of what happened to Mum?'

Rufus's blue eyes flashed, giving Spike a glimpse of the man he'd once feared. 'This has nothing to do with your *theories* about your mother,' he retorted. 'No,' he went on, 'because of his religion. They all make a song and dance of it out here, but David was the real deal. A staunch Roman Catholic, far more devoted than your mother. Those religious paintings he loved . . . He really *believed* in their message, that suicide is a cardinal sin. And who would choose to go to hell?'

Someone who was already there, Spike wanted to say, but didn't.

'And as for what they're claiming he did to Teresa. His beloved Teresa . . . It's an abominable slur.'

'Perhaps he was ill.'

'David was one of the sanest men I ever met. To a fault. Always such a *planner*,' Rufus continued, shaking his head. 'Working on his catalogues, plodding along. David wasn't spontaneous. Bloody-minded, yes. Delusions of grandeur, maybe. But *this*?' Spike felt his father's dry, bony fingers squeeze the back of his hand. 'You'll look into it, won't you, son? You'll find out what happened.'

'Yes, Dad. Now come on. I'll run you a hot bath.'

7

Spike checked the temperature of the bathwater, then turned back to the open door. His father was propped up in bed in a white hotel robe, devouring a club sandwich with the sort of rapacity which sometimes made Spike wonder how ill he really was. Spread over his knees was a tourist magazine that had come free with the room. 'Listen to this,' Rufus said, folding a fistful of fries into his mouth. 'On 15 April 1942, the entire civilian population of Malta was awarded the George Cross for enduring 154 days of continuous German and Italian bombardment.' Rufus lifted up the magazine. 'This is page four, son. We had the Great Siege on page two, when Malta apparently saved the whole of Europe from Muslim rule. Not shy in coming forward, are they?'

Spike glanced down at his father's empty water glass. 'Have you taken your beta blockers?'

'How many sieges has Gibraltar withstood?' Rufus asked, picking up the bottle of water.

Spike smiled. 'Fourteen.'

'Fourteen sieges,' Rufus said, swallowing down two pills. 'Moors, Spaniards, U-boats ... You don't hear us crowing, do you?'

'Never.'

After steering his father to the bathroom, Spike stripped down to his boxers, staring out at the wooden balcony which protruded over the small city square below. What was it with the Maltese and balconies? Something to do with medieval times, Spike seemed to remember, when the Arabs had ruled the islands – allowing well-born women to observe street life unseen. 'Do you remember Michael Malaspina?' he called through.

'Who?' Reclining in the bath, Rufus resembled a skeleton soaking in acid.

'Michael Malaspina,' Spike repeated.

Rufus's silver mane of hair was dampened back, pale blue eyes blinking, like a nocturnal animal torn from its burrow. 'You mean the Baron?'

'He's invited us to dinner.'

'Then we must go,' Rufus said, dipping his head back into the water.

Back in the bedroom, Spike picked up his uncle's diary and lay down. Just one week before David died, he'd been to Gozo, Malta's smaller sister island, visiting Our Lady of St Agatha – a church by the sound of it. He turned the page. The day after David's death, he'd scheduled a meeting at the Co-Cathedral of St John with the chief curator. A receipt was stapled to the page: photographs awaiting collection. The next week, an appointment with someone called Olsa . . .

'Son?' came a voice from next door. 'I can't seem to get the cap off this. *Son?*'

Cursing to himself, Spike closed the diary and stood.

✠

The man lies bare-chested on the bed. From the street below come the sounds of cars, restaurants, chatter. The man stares upwards. The display on his new sound system casts green lozenges of light on the ceiling. He feels his ribcage rise and fall; soothed by the rhythm, he dares to close his eyes.

Beneath his lids, the parade of faces begins again. The women emerge one by one through a curtain. Once at the centre of the stage, they turn their heads, their expressions the same: bored, neutral, until they blink, and their eyes grow larger, black as night, blood seeping from the corners, dripping down painted cheeks. An older woman appears. She wears a blue dressing gown. Clutched to her chest is a baby . . .

The man snaps open his eyes. The ceiling is darker, the voices outside louder; he hears female laughter carry up on the breeze. He touches his forehead. Warm and sticky; fumbling for the lamp he finds not blood, but perspiration.

Rolling out of bed, the man picks up the remote and switches on the music, waiting for the hard, thrash metal to cleanse his thoughts. Head clearer, he steps forward to the full-length mirror which hangs on the bedroom cupboard. Looping a hand over one shoulder, he twists his neck, admiring his tattoo. The inky skin is taut and smooth. He straightens up, then dresses carefully for the evening ahead.

Chapter Three

A posse of men loitered outside the charity office, each holding a hand-painted placard. 'Close All Tent Camps' read one. Another was more direct: 'Blacks Go Home'. The men's chests were swollen with a heavy, filled-out look which might have been fat or might have been muscle. As they shook their placards at Spike's approach, their biceps suggested the latter.

The charity office door was emblazoned with stickers – Red Cross, Salvation Army, Save the Children – like a mid-market restaurant advertising its modest success. Inside, Spike made out a figure in the gloom, standing with folded arms. He knocked on the glass with a knuckle. The figure moved towards the door.

Spike turned to the protesters – 'Don't panic. He appears to be Caucasian' – as the door opened to a young man in khaki chinos and a white Brooks Brothers shirt.

'*Pulizïa?*' the man said in Maltese, and even Spike could tell he was not a native speaker.

'Teresa's nephew.'

The man opened the door wide enough for Spike to slip through, then locked it again behind him to a chorus of guttural Maltese protests.

The man turned from the door. Beneath his side-parted hair, his square-jawed face wore a sprinkling of reddish freckles across the nose. Spike imagined him advertising milk, or fortified bread. 'I called the cops, like, an *hour* ago,' he said in an inevitably American accent. 'That new placard is straight-up inflammatory – actionable, even.' He swept his ash-blond fringe aside with the palm of a hand. 'Apologies,' he went on, 'rude of me. My name's John Petrovic.'

'Is that Serbian?'

John smiled. 'Not since Ellis Island. The family's mostly Scotch and Irish these days. Why do you ask?'

'Doesn't matter. I'm Spike Sanguinetti.'

'So sad about Teresa,' John said as he crossed the office. 'May the Lord rest and take mercy upon her soul.' He closed his green eyes, as though allowing the blessing a moment to wend its way up to heaven. His long fair lashes curled up at the ends.

'May I?' Spike said, motioning to the strip lights.

John snapped open his eyes. 'Sure. Didn't want to encourage those goons by letting them know I was here.'

Two plastic bins stood by the far wall, printed sheets of paper taped to their rims: 'CLOTHING', 'TINNED FOOD'. The former contained a few T-shirts, the latter was empty.

'We're all still reeling,' John said as he sat down at his desk. 'You're here for the funeral, I guess?'

'Funerals.'

'What? Oh, yeah. Right.'

John pursed his lips in a manner that suggested the Lord's blessing might not be extended to Teresa's husband, then consulted a heavy-looking diver's wristwatch. 'Cops don't even bother turning up these days,' he muttered. 'We're totally off their radar.' He turned back to Spike, as though taking him in properly for the first time. 'Anyway. How can I help?'

'I'm trying to understand how this could have happened.'

'How what could have happened?'

'To the Mifsuds.' Spike paused. 'Did Teresa seem herself to you?'

'She was a bit strung out by our friends outside. Every day, new people – it's like they're working on shift. But otherwise she was OK. The girls loved her, she was great at her work –'

'Did she only teach women?'

'We have four migrant centres on the island,' John said, relaxing into his chair and his subject. 'The first was founded in Marsa, on the site of an old technical college. That's all male. Then, when that reached capacity, they opened a new one at Hal Far, in a former British army barracks. The number of women increased, so they opened a dedicated female block. Then nature took its course and we got a family centre up the road.'

'And Teresa only taught at the women's centre?'

John nodded. 'English and cultural orientation.'

'Can I go there?'

'Not without clearance.'

'Can you take me?'

'I'm on housekeeping,' John said, looking down at the remarkably uncluttered desk.

'Is there anyone else?'

'Our two full-time teachers are on holiday, the only one left is –'

There was a rap at the glass. 'Right on cue,' John said with a smile. He got to his feet and unlocked the door.

Another snatch of protest from outside as the door closed. 'Fucking Neanderthals,' came a familiar husky voice. 'Hey, you,' John said, pecking the new arrival on each cheek. Spike heard the sound of a handbag dumped on the floor.

'This is Teresa's nephew,' John said. 'Name of –' He broke off, sensing something in the atmosphere.

'Hello, Spike,' Zahra said.

Spike's dislike of Malta's newfangled buses intensified as he found tourists were charged double the fare. Taking a seat in an empty row, he glanced across the aisle at Zahra. Her hair was cut in a sleek black bob, hooked behind her elfin ears. Her narrow eyes and the dark sweep of her cheekbones caused Spike a familiar sense of turbulence. He dug the edge of his hand into his stomach to chase it away. 'Unusual guy. What is he, Mormon?'

Zahra turned towards him. 'I'm so sorry about Teresa, Spike. And your uncle.'

Spike looked away. The bus was gathering speed, driving on the left, a colonialist throwback even Gibraltar didn't share. Flanking the road, drystone walls gave onto a patchwork quilt of fields, some grazing sheep, others planted with bushy rows of vines. Every thirty yards or so stood lone African men, watching the traffic pass as they chewed on some kind of leaf – khat, perhaps.

A pickup truck had stopped ahead; Spike watched the hirsute Maltese driver beckon from his window to a gangly black man, who detached himself from the wall and climbed over the tailgate. A similar transaction was going on round the next corner: day labourers plying for casual work, Spike thought, remembering photos from school textbooks covering the Great Depression.

The bus turned down a potholed track. A group of young Africans was coming along the verge, dressed in knock-off labels and texting on mobile phones. Still seated, Zahra tied a sequinned headscarf over her shining hair, then pressed the bell. The bus drew to a halt, engine throbbing.

3

Spike followed Zahra along the rubbish-strewn verge. A jumbo jet roared overhead, wheels down like a woodwasp's legs. Spike didn't remember this view from the plane window yesterday: the flight path must lie directly above the camps, no doubt to prevent the tourists from seeing what lay beneath their feet. To the right rose a tower marking the start of an airport runway.

Zahra was carrying a laundry sack containing the charity's meagre clothing donations on one shoulder, her handbag on the other. 'Let me help,' said Spike.

'I can manage.'

The group of Africans approached. The youth in front wore a hooded leather jacket; he muttered something to Zahra in what sounded like Arabic. She threw back a retort, making him stop slack-jawed as his companions gave a whoop of delight.

A chicken-wire fence appeared to the left. Through creeper-entwined mesh, Spike watched some men playing football in the scrub. He heard a collective groan as the ball fired wide of make-shift goalposts.

The undergrowth began to thin, and Spike made out the first tent. He'd been imagining something which could be rolled into a rucksack, but this was an enormous white marquee, four-sided with a lofty, pitched roof. Similar tents stretched beyond; it might have been some kind of trade fair, but for the torn canvas and stink of human faeces. 'How many inmates are there?' Spike asked.

'They're not inmates; they come and go as they please.'

'How many?'

'Seven thousand at the last count.'

'And the population of Malta is . . . ?'

'About four hundred thousand.' Zahra glanced over at Spike as she walked. 'None of them wants to be here, Spike. They're all trying to get to Italy. They get blown off course.'

'It beats prison, I suppose.'

'That comes first. Between six weeks and a year in detention on the other side of the island. Then they get temporary visas and are moved to the tent camps.'

'How long can they stay?'

'However long it takes to assess each case. Some get deported, the lucky few get EU passports.'

'What are the criteria?'

'I thought you were the lawyer.'

'You were my only immigration case.'

Zahra looked down at her shoes, then continued. 'If they're economic migrants, they usually get sent home. If there's a war going on in their country, or a famine, they're classed as refugees and can stay. The Germans have been taking some –'

'The Germans?'

'In exchange for Malta supporting them in the EU.'

Spike saw a cat's cradle of washing lines strung between the tents. 'Must be a lot of wars on at the moment.'

'The Arab Spring.'

'Still?'

'The deportations are expensive. You need to charter a plane, enlist two security guards per migrant.'

'Who pays?'

'Maltese taxes.'

'Hence the protests at your office?'

'The economic climate doesn't help.'

They came into a forecourt with a Portakabin at one end. Three cars with Maltese plates were parked in front. 'Wait here,' Zahra said.

Two separate camps adjoined the car park, one where Spike had seen the football players, another from which a tall woman in a headscarf was exiting to join a line of youths outside the Portakabin. An older man appeared by the queue, swaying as though drunk. He stumbled up to the youths, who ignored him, except for one who shoved him in the chest when he came too close. Still rocking back and forth, the man began to focus his attention on Spike, then wandered unsteadily over. '*Fonu*,' he said, moving from foot to foot. An open wound festered in the corner of his mouth.

'Just English or Spanish,' Spike said. 'A bit of Italian.'

'*Té-lé-phone*,' the man said in a French accent. 'I call to Mali. For my mother.'

'He is sick,' one of the youths called over, then made a pelvic thrust, to the amusement of his friends.

Spike delved into a pocket. 'What's the number?'

The sight of the phone seemed to sober the man up, and he reached out a hand. His left thumbnail was uncut, curly and opaque.

'I'll be back in twenty minutes,' Spike said, passing him the phone. 'Keep it brief.'

Zahra was standing in the Portakabin doorway, the sack of clothes gone from her shoulder. 'I hope that was pay-as-you-go,' she said as Spike climbed the front steps.

A worn-looking supervisor sat behind the desk. He said something to Zahra in Maltese; her reply suggested she'd already mastered the language.

'You wanna visit the female camp?' the supervisor asked Spike.

'Yes.'

'ID.'

Spike handed over a Supreme Court of Gibraltar security card. The supervisor slammed it in a drawer without a glance.

'Has he received medical help?'

'Who?'

'That man.'

'For syphilis?' The supervisor gave a laugh. 'It comes and goes.'

'But a doctor –'

'Yes, yes,' the supervisor said. 'The doctor is here each night.' He snatched up the phone, coughing into the receiver. A young

North African sat in a plastic chair at the edge of the cabin, paper form wilting in one hand; Spike and Zahra walked past him to a side door.

There was little to betoken a classroom: loose chairs rather than desks, a table at the front with a tired pile of children's books. On the wall, a poster designated each letter of the alphabet with an animal: Alligator for A, Butterfly for B. Spike checked automatically for X and saw the inevitable fudge: eX-tinct, with a sad-eyed image of a dinosaur.

Zahra straightened a few chairs, then pressed in the bar of a security door. They stepped out into a large fenced-off area. In front spread two tents; ranged to the side was a series of rusty corrugated shipping containers. Two women were exiting a doorway which had been soldered into the nearest. 'Did they run out of tents?' Spike asked.

'Three years ago.'

A circle of women sat on upturned paint pots heating a vat of water over an open fire. Spike caught a whiff of something caramelising in the embers: sweet potato, perhaps, or carrots. An older woman was pegging washing on a line, while two more stood by the chicken-wire fence, chatting to some men on the other side. Spike heard a distant cheer: a goal, at last, for the footballers.

'Seen enough?'

'Did Teresa teach any of these women?'

'I don't know. This isn't my camp.'

One of the younger girls rose to her feet and shouted into the container. Another woman emerged. A moment later, six of them were gathered round Zahra. 'Dinah?' one of them said.

Zahra replied in Arabic, and the eldest woman raised a hand to her face. Zahra stepped back, undoing her headscarf, shaking free her inky-black bob. The women spoke to one another urgently.

'What's going on?' Spike said.

'I don't know,' Zahra replied, edging away and directing a question at the younger girls. 'They thought I was someone else,' she said to Spike once she'd heard the answer.

'Who?'

'A friend.'

'Dinah?' Spike said.

'Dinah,' one of the girls repeated. 'She tall girl. Pretty like she.'

'You speak good English,' Spike said. 'Did Teresa teach you?'

'Teresa. Nice lady.'

'They don't know she's dead,' Zahra said quickly as she refastened her headscarf.

'Can you ask them if they ever met Teresa's husband?'

Zahra spoke again in Arabic. 'No,' she translated back.

'Did they see her with another man?'

'Why?'

'Just ask.'

She spoke again. 'They're saying the handsome American. That's –'

'John,' Spike interrupted. 'Can you ask them if –'

'You can ask *me*,' Zahra said. 'John used to drive me and Teresa home after work. Any further questions?' She turned abruptly and continued talking to the girls in Arabic.

Spike walked away to one of the tents. The nearest end was open, lines of rags stretching over the lumpy ground, covering the indeterminate shapes of what looked like corpses. A reek of old urine sharpened the air; in one corner lay a picture book with a yellow duck on the front. As Spike peered in further, he saw one of the corpse figures rise up, a haggard leathery face staring from beneath a shroud. He raised a hand in greeting, but the figure slumped back down.

Shaking his head, Spike walked back to Zahra, who was standing alone, jotting something in a notebook. 'Do the press know about this place?'

'Of course.'

'It's outrageous.'

'Spoken like a true tourist.' She put the notebook back in her bag.

'What were you writing down?'

'Their friend's gone missing.'

'Is that unusual?'

'Not really; people skip across to Sicily the whole time.'

'So why the sudden interest?'

'Apparently she's just had a baby. No one's heard from her since last week.'

'Wouldn't she have moved to the family camp?'

Zahra gave a weary sigh. 'That's what I'm going to find out.'

They exited via a smaller gateway to the forecourt. 'Why were you asking all those questions, anyway?' Zahra said.

'Just a concerned nephew.'

'You've been listening to the gossip, right? Well, it's bullshit. Teresa would never have cheated on David. She told me once that she had never thought she would get married. That she'd missed her chance. She felt blessed to have found him.'

Spike stopped. 'How are you getting back to Valletta?'

'I have a lesson to teach.'

'And then?'

'I'll get a lift.'

'From the handsome American?'

'We're going for a drink.'

'Drowning your sorrows?'

'Sticking together. It's been tough.'

'Which bar?'

'Pasha.'

'Sounds like an ideal place to mourn.'

Zahra set off towards the Portakabin, then stopped. 'I'll see you at the funeral, Spike,' she called back.

Spike headed for the gate, then remembered his ID and returned to the Portakabin. On his way out, he paused by the side door, staring in at the classroom. Five women now occupied the chairs, each with a child on their lap. Two were breastfeeding. At the front, Zahra was holding up a sheet of A4 paper in lieu of a blackboard. A clumsily drawn car, a stickman family beside it. Zahra said something, and Spike heard the chant of the women repeating it. She was focusing so intently she didn't see him peering in.

Outside, a figure was sitting on the wall by the road, picking at the sores around his mouth with a long curly thumbnail.

'Hello,' Spike said.

The man glanced up. Opening his hand, he revealed Spike's slim mobile phone. '*Je m'appelle Frankie*,' he said. '*Comme Frank Sinatra, uh?*'

Spike took the phone. Just one call made, he saw as he walked away – duration three minutes.

A bus was parked ahead on the verge. In a nod to the *ancien régime*, a sticker had found its way onto the windscreen. '*The driver carries no cash*,' it said, with the pay-off below, '*he's married.*'

Spike bought a single ticket back to town.

4

Spike picked up a portion of deep-fried dates from the kiosk by the bus terminus. The pain-au-chocolat-shaped package was dripping with oil, but its dark chewy centre was honeyed and delicious. Behind him ran the St James Ditch, the moat built to protect the land approach to Valletta from attack. People kept coming and going over its walkway: language students, lawyers, disaffected Africans.

A black, low-slung motorbike drew up on the other side of the walkway. The driver dismounted, helmet on, as Spike checked the time: 10.40 a.m. He knew he ought to be pressing on with the business of probate – filling in the grant of representation, establishing debts, life insurance, beneficiaries – but instead he dug into a trouser pocket and pulled out his uncle's diary.

The man on the motorcycle was still watching. Something about him prompted unease: the sun was warmer now, yet he'd kept his helmet on. As soon as Spike started walking towards him, he swung a leg over his bike and gunned the engine into the suburb of Floriana.

5

In the square outside the Co-Cathedral of St John, a ponytailed South American had set up a stall selling CDs of pan-pipe music. Tootling from a battery-powered stereo was an Andean version of 'Buffalo Soldier'. The man gazed at Spike with hopeful, off-season eyes as he walked past him up the cathedral steps.

'I have a meeting with the chief curator,' Spike said, holding up his uncle's diary.

'You'll have to buy a ticket like everyone else,' the woman at the counter replied curtly.

Six euros for entrance, another twenty to join a tour that was already under way. Vatican, Inc. must be turning a tidy profit.

Spike pushed through a turnstile into the interior of the cathedral. The usual baroque excess: golden sunbeams exploding from the backs of saintly heads, frescoed ceilings, gilt cornices, tablets on the floor depicting the skeletons of those buried beneath. Piped choral music came from hidden speakers as a few visitors milled about, struggling to decipher their guidebooks in the dim light.

From the oratory at the edge of the nave, Spike heard clipped female tones. The baroque found a new pinnacle in this small, high-ceilinged annexe. It was clear where the main attraction lay: a group of tourists was gathered together as a woman held forth in English, gesturing towards a painting above the altar.

Spike moved closer, sliding the rope soles of his espadrilles over the worn, inlaid marble. The canvas was almost the size of a city billboard. It showed a stone wall, with a barred window on the right-hand side, through which two grimy-faced prisoners were peering into a courtyard below. In the foreground, a heavily muscled, bare-chested man was bending to a figure splayed on the mud-packed ground. Judging by the hue of the figure's skin, he was already dead. As Spike drew closer, he saw blood spilling from a recently slit throat, hands tied behind back. The executioner was gripping the figure's hair, preparing to complete the decapitation with a razor blade. A maid stooped alongside with a dish to receive the head, as a thickly bearded jailer stood behind, holding a set of keys, open-mouthed as he issued instructions. The only member of the group showing any emotion was an elderly woman, hands clasped over her ears, presumably to blot out the dead man's screams.

'When Michelangelo Merisi da Caravaggio first came to Malta in 1607 –' The tour guide broke off as Spike approached. She was an attractive woman in her early forties with wavy, shoulder-length dark hair. A neat ski-jump nose was topped off by a pair of chunky black-rimmed specs.

'Sorry,' Spike mouthed. 'Running late.'

The tour guide peered over the frame of her glasses. Her low-cut silk blouse was lent a degree of demureness by an expertly knotted Hermès scarf. Her petite legs looked toned in gleaming stockings and kitten heels. 'Where was I?' she said.

'In 1607?' offered an eager American.

Glancing again at Spike, the tour guide returned to the painting. 'In 1607, Caravaggio was on the run after murdering a pimp in Naples. Why would the Holy Order of St John harbour a notorious criminal and womaniser? Why would this brotherhood of Christian soldiers compromise their strict codes of piety and chastity to take him in? Here, in *The Beheading of St John the Baptist*, we find our answer.'

Spike followed the group's gaze. Light illuminated the Baptist's body from above; Spike looked for a window or open roof, but its source was unclear.

'Talent,' the tour guide said with a smile. 'The knights had to decorate their new city, so Caravaggio and the Grand Master struck a bargain. Caravaggio would produce religious works of art, such as this depiction of the order's patron saint, in return for which he would become a knight, so gaining redemption in the eyes of God, and a pardon, he hoped, from the Pope in Rome. The knights received their masterpieces at a discount, and Caravaggio got his salvation. A win–win situation. Or so it seemed.' The tour guide lowered her voice stagily. 'See the blood streaming from the Baptist's neck?'

The Americans crowded closer.

'At the base, the words "F. Michelangelo" – "Fra" – or "Brother" – "Michelangelo" – are written in black in the blood. As well as being the largest painting Caravaggio produced, it's also the only one he signed. You can see how proud he was to have become a knight. Alas, the mutually beneficial arrangement was not to last.'

The tour guide stepped back to a pinboard of photographs. 'Here in the oratory, in the very room where Caravaggio received his knighthood, where his masterpiece, *The Beheading*, still hung, he was defrocked *in absentia* by the order. Why? An altercation with a brother knight in a tavern in Valletta. Caravaggio's violent nature won through. The order had him imprisoned in Fort San Angelo, just south of here, but he managed to escape by boat to Italy, where he died not long afterwards of fever.' She pointed up at a print of an engraving. 'Here we see an image of the Venerable

Council of the Order convening for a criminal trial. The same body would have met to expel Caravaggio; in the centre would have sat Grand Master de Wignacourt, whom Caravaggio had captured in a personal portrait only a few months previously . . .'

Spike moved back to the main event, staring up at the blood spilling from the martyr's neck. 'No flash photography,' hissed a security guard, alerted by his sudden focus. When he rejoined the main group, the guide was pointing at a less dramatic canvas at the other end of the oratory.

'All the Maltese Caravaggios are now abroad, save for two, *The Beheading of St John*, which you have just seen, and here, the less famous but equally exquisite *St Jerome Writing*. Some of you may recall that for a while we lost one of these masterpieces. See, to the left of the scribe's hand, damage incurred when the paint-ing was stolen in 1984. Pieces of the canvas were mailed back in order to try and secure a ransom. Thankfully it was recovered after an extensive police operation.'

'Who took it?' asked an American.

'The thieves were never brought to justice. But don't forget, Malta is only eighty kilometres south of Sicily.'

Polite chuckles; Spike looked up and saw a black CCTV camera peering down from the doorway.

'The use of chiaroscuro, literally "light-dark", gives a famously theatrical quality to Caravaggio's work, which . . .'

Once the tour guide had wound things up, Spike went over. 'May I have a word?'

She tilted her head.

'It's about David Mifsud.'

Her smile died. 'Ten minutes,' she said, before turning back to the Americans.

6

Spike exited the cathedral past racks of overpriced religious tat into a graveyard giving onto the street. Sitting down on a wooden bench, he caught strains of a pan-pipe version of 'My Heart Will Go On' filtering through the railings.

The tour group began filing out, the more inquisitive pausing to read the knights' crumbling gravestones, then giving up as they registered their illegibility. At last the chief curator appeared. She glanced about uneasily, then set off up the path.

Spike stood as she approached. He'd been intending to accompany her wherever she was going, but she swept her hands down the back of her herringbone-check skirt and sat down.

He retook his seat. 'I'm Spike Sanguinetti.'

'Rachel Cassar.'

They shook hands sideways.

'David was my uncle.'

'I can see the resemblance. And you're from . . . ?'

'Gibraltar.'

She looked puzzled.

'My maternal grandparents were Maltese. They emigrated to Gibraltar after World War II. When Malta became independent, David moved back. My mother stayed on.'

'Sanguinetti sounds Italian.'

'My father's family were merchants from Genoa. Many generations ago.'

Rachel's scarf slipped a fraction from her shoulder; she lifted it back in place. 'I presume you're here for the money.'

Spike paused, then gave a non-committal smile.

'I've already made out the cheque to David, but I can easily write another. I'm not sure what one does in these situations.'

'So David was working for you?'

She nodded, smoothing the front of her skirt over her thighs.

'And that was why you were scheduled to meet last week? To settle up?'

'He didn't come to the meeting, so I left it to him to get in touch. Then a few days later I read about what had happened in *The Times*. Just the most awful shock.' Behind her glasses, Spike saw her dark brown eyes brim with tears.

'What kind of work was he doing for you?'

'We have a reserve collection at the National Museum of Fine Arts.' She nodded as he offered her a handkerchief. 'Minor and damaged works. David was cataloguing them.'

'And he'd finished?'

She dabbed at the corners of her eyes, then passed the handkerchief back. 'Three months ago. The meeting was to iron out any final issues. Then he was going to retire.'

'How did he feel about that?'

'I'm not sure ... I suppose I thought he might return to his roots.'

'Meaning?'

'Well ... you know he trained as an artist. He was quite talented actually – particularly his still lifes in oil. When he was in his thirties, I believe he put on an exhibition in Valletta. Sadly very few paintings sold. They were too old-fashioned; the wrong register. So he leapt completely to the other extreme. Pursued an academic route at the University of Malta. But that was David ... Of course, you must know all this already.'

'Not really.'

Rachel gave him a look.

'We weren't close.'

'I see. Well, he threw himself into the art world as much as Malta allows – curating the odd exhibition, writing articles in the local magazines. We used him at the museum whenever we could. He was extremely knowledgeable.'

'Did he seem depressed to you?'

'I don't know if depressed is the word . . . Dispirited, maybe. There was always a sense that the work was beneath him. Which it was, in a sense. Though recently . . .'

'What?'

Spike saw her roll her eyes to the right, remembering. 'Well, I wasn't *that* surprised when he didn't turn up for the meeting. He'd seemed a bit distracted lately. As though he had something else on his mind.'

'Something other than the work he was doing for you?'

'Yes. He'd seemed . . . excited, almost.'

'About what?'

She shrugged, scarf slipping again. This time she let it lie. 'At our last meeting in the museum he had a bit of a spring in his step. Normally he was quite formal. But when he arrived that time, he kissed me on both cheeks. Then as he left, he kind of . . .' She smiled, flushing slightly. 'Well . . . he was nearly as tall as you. He practically picked me up.'

'Do you think he was on something?'

'How do you mean?'

'Antidepressants.'

'I'm not a doctor, Mr Sanguinetti.'

'What about Teresa? Were they happy?'

Rachel frowned. 'We never spoke about his personal life.'

'But when you saw them together they . . .'

'Seemed fine.' She paused. 'But who knows what really goes on in a relationship.'

Spike glanced automatically at her left hand: no wedding ring. She followed his eyes. 'I'd better get back,' she said, standing.

'Thanks for taking the time to talk to me.'

'A pleasure. It's been on my mind. So, do you want me to make out the cheque to you?'

'Leave it to Teresa's charity.'

Spike thought he caught a flash of disapproval. They shook hands; now it was Rachel whose eyes dipped to Spike's fingers.

'One more thing,' Spike called out.

She stopped, hand on hip.

'When David was cataloguing the reserve collection, what sort of work did it involve?'

Her face fell a little. 'Provenance, first and foremost. Visits to the archives. Fact-checking, really.'

'Photographs?'

'That's always the starting point.' She half turned away.

'Had he taken all the photographs he needed?'

'Yes, and we'd set them into the catalogue. Why?'

'No reason. Goodbye.'

Spike set off back to the street, opening up his uncle's diary as he walked and tearing out the receipt for the print shop. Whatever these photographs were, they didn't relate to work David had been doing for Rachel Cassar.

7

The Omertà Photographic Centre lay midway down a dingy triq on the western fringe of Valletta. The shops on either side were boarded up: even UNESCO World Heritage Sites had their run-down neighbourhoods. A small copper bell above the door tinkled as Spike pushed through a veil of multicoloured ribbons. He handed the print slip to an obese man with a beard, who rolled reluctantly off his stool to go to the back of the shop.

A few moments later, the man returned with a thick sleeve of photographs. 'Two hundred and eighty-three euros,' he said flatly.

Spike looked up in surprise. 'Christ! How much was my last set?'

'What was the name again?'

'Dr David Mifsud.'

As the man bent to his computer screen, Spike peered inside the pack of photos. The first few were blurred black-and-white smudges. Mifsud may have been an artist but he was no photographer.

'No previous jobs on record,' the man said.

'How about for the National Museum of Fine Arts?'

The man sighed and returned to the screen. 'Nothing.'

Spike paid up and left. The sun had dipped behind a cloud: there was better light at the end of the triq, so he walked along the cobblestones, emerging at the edge of the St James Ditch. He looked down over the protective wall and saw what looked like a dried riverbed fifty feet below: bin bags, cacti clumps, an open-topped skip where some builders appeared to have been repairing the foundations.

Facing outwards, Spike laid the sleeve of photos on top of the wall. More of the same black-and-white smears, each with a date in the corner, 16 January, two weeks before Mifsud's death. He flipped through further: he'd just spent the thick end of three hundred euros on some out-of-focus prints.

As he turned over the next photo, he stopped. This time the image was clearer. It showed an oval-shaped painting, still in its frame: in the centre stood a dark-skinned woman, her brown hair tied in a loose knot at her nape, her arms above her head, her wrists shackled to a ringbolt on what looked like a cell wall. Her dress had been pulled down, dangling by her waist. Alongside her stood a man in leather breeches, a pair of bolt cutters in his hands.

Spike tilted the photo to the light. The woman's left breast had been cut off, blood streaming down her midriff. The jaws of the cutters were clasped around her right breast, ready to slice again.

So lost was Spike in grim fascination – the jailer's business-like expression, the woman's semi-conscious face – that he didn't hear the sound of a motorbike pulling up behind him.

8

As Spike turned over the next photograph, he felt something smash into the small of his back. His groin collided with the low wall in front. He managed to sweep most of the photographs behind him, but a few slipped over the edge, fluttering down into the void.

Hands pressed to the top of the wall, he tried to push himself backwards, but the weight on his spine was too great. His heels began to rise from the ground; now his head was leaning out over the wall. He twisted his neck, glimpsing something shiny at the periphery of his vision. The pressure increased; his chest was now protruding over the edge, just his toes on the ground. 'Wait,' he gasped.

'Go home, foreigner,' came a whispered voice.

Spike caught a sweet smell on the man's breath. 'OK,' he said, as the photographs still zigzagged downwards, finally landing in the builders' skip, 'OK, OK . . .'

The force reduced, and for the first time Spike felt pain where his palms had been digging into the top of the wall. As soon as his heels touched the ground, he swung an arm backwards, swivelling with his hip for maximum impact. His elbow hit something hard. He clutched it to his chest, stumbling away from the wall.

The man was walking casually back to his motorbike. He wore blue canvas trousers and a white T-shirt. Over his head was a black helmet. As he hoisted a leg over the bike, Spike caught sight of a strong, grizzled jaw.

The man smiled, then slid down his visor and drove away. As soon as he was gone, Spike bent down and gathered the remaining photographs.

✳

The boy adjusts the vice, then steps away from the head. The entire four-foot length of the unicorn's horn is now coated in a transparent gum; the boy attaches a line of silver ribbon to the base, then begins winding it up around the papier-mâché cone, trying to keep the spiral even as he moves steadily upwards to the point.

His mind turns again to this evening's plans: meeting Luisa Camilleri in Paceville. What if she prefers Anthony to him? He knows Anthony will not hesitate.

Still circling the head, the boy passes by the warehouse wall. A low, bestial grunting vibrates through the brickwork. The boy stops, then continues his work, arms rising higher as he walks.

He stops again. The animal sounds have returned, followed by a distant high-pitched wail, like a child's scream. The boy feels his heart start to beat; dropping the silver thread, he goes to the doorway and pushes it open.

It is dark outside; he is meeting Luisa in less than an hour. A breeze is blowing through the masts of the boats ahead, creating a soft wail; as the boy turns back to the warehouse, he sees shadows cast by the finished Carnival floats: the flame of a dragon, the jaws of a lion. In the centre, the huge head of the unicorn still sits in its vice, decapitated, ribbon dripping from its horn like silver blood.

Quelling his unease, the boy flicks off the lights and steps outside, pulling the door behind him. His hand shakes as he fumbles for the padlock.

He strides away along the concrete. Another squall of wind rattles the ships' rigging; a few yards on, he slows, chiding himself for behaving like an infant, wondering what Luisa would think if she could see him now. By the time he is climbing the steps back up to the road, he has forgotten the noises, his thoughts already on the rich possibilities of the night ahead.

Chapter Four

I

'So I thought why spare the horses?' Rufus said. 'Mercedes hearse. Three-car cortège. Hundred white lilies. You only get one send-off, after all.'

As they approached Triq Sant'Orsla, Spike's eye was caught by a statue adorning the street corner. A bare-chested woman staring up at the sky, both breasts missing.

'No doubt the estate will cover it, but in the meantime, I wondered if . . . son?'

Feeling a touch on his elbow, Spike started a little, then turned to his father. Long white hair pushed back from his brow, Rufus wore his best dark suit, lightened by a mauve Gibraltar Heritage Committee tie, an institution of which he was chairman.

Spike exhaled, then pointed to the statue. 'Do you know who that represents, Dad?'

'Whom what represents?' Rufus said, fumbling in his pocket for his bifocals.

'Never mind. You were saying?'

They continued along the cobbles. Spike still hadn't told his father about the attack by the St James Ditch. Hadn't told anyone, in fact. A case of mistaken identity, he repeated dubiously to himself as he reached into the pocket of his jeans and checked his phone. Still no reply from Zahra.

'. . . of course the big question is the venue for the wake. While I think the Phoenicia *would* be nice, it's not exactly –'

'Dad?'

Rufus was standing outside the Mifsud flat. Realising his mistake, he turned and joined Spike by the entrance to Palazzo Malaspina. A Maltese flag dangled from the oak-framed door, a George Cross on its left-hand side beside the phrase, *For Gallantry*.

Rufus shook his head in disapproval, then reached for the pomegranate knocker.

2

The Malaspina maid was surprisingly young and attractive, squeezed into a hi-vis anorak as though interrupted en route for a bike ride. She pointed apathetically at the dark curving staircase which dominated the hallway. Rufus went first, gripping the mahogany banister with long, splayed fingers. Spike followed behind.

Rufus took it one step at a time. He refused to walk with a cane despite the doctors' insistence that the ligaments in his legs could give way at any point. A fall Spike could catch: it was the possibility that Rufus's aorta might split in two that worried him. The democratic nature of Marfan syndrome: all connective tissue equally at risk.

'Almost there . . .' Rufus said as he neared the landing.

Upstairs, two life-size portraits hung on either side of a double-doored entrance. On the right-hand wall stood a younger Baron Malaspina, captured in front of a bookcase, his right hand cupping his left elbow, his three-piece suit and waxed moustache suggesting a touch of the dandy in his early years. On the other side of the door frame, straight-backed in a Louis Quinze chair, sat the Baroness. Spike was reminded of the unusual beauty which even as a child had moved him. Golden hair snaking over bare shoulders, pale oval face with a heart-shaped mouth, the narrow hips and long svelte legs of a dancer ... There was a reason she was seated, Spike thought – five in fact, one for each inch she towered over her husband.

One might have taken their union as a straightforward transaction of looks and status, except that the Baroness's family was said to outrank even her husband's. Her mother had been a young Russian aristocrat, evacuated by the British after the Bolshevik revolution, arriving in Malta on HMS *Marlborough* in 1919 as part of a convoy of White Russian refugees. The Russian connection had been maintained by the Baroness teaching ballet in the years before she'd met her husband.

'Hel-lo?' came a shrill voice from behind the doorway.

'It's only us,' Spike called back.

As the doors opened, Spike glanced from portrait to subject: the Baroness's cheekbones were more pronounced, her skin more parchment-like, yet she remained a beauty.

'My darlinks!'

Rufus was drawn into the Baroness's floating chiffon dress, freezing like a cat in a child's embrace. As he pulled away, Spike saw a touch of pinkness in his face.

'And you,' the Baroness said, turning to Spike. 'Michael forewarned me, but what a man you have become.' She pecked him on both cheeks, trailing a rose-scented powder. 'Like that matinee idol of the forties, the Spaniard, so rangy and handsome, but with those eyes ...' She glanced back at Rufus. 'Why, you have given him your blue eyes, Rufus! If I were only twenty years younger. Or five!'

The maid was waiting on the stairs, mouth set. 'Off you go, Clara,' the Baroness snapped, before wafting inside past the image of her younger self.

Rufus remained swaying on the landing; placing a hand on the small of his back, Spike encouraged him inside the drawing room. Frayed rugs lay seemingly at random over uneven oak floorboards; tucked against one wall was a harpsichord, its cypress-wood lid decorated with pastoral scenes. Tall windows gave onto an inner courtyard, orange trees growing from below, pressing their leaves to the glass as though seeking to eavesdrop. The central coffee table was piled with Russian art books, enclosed on three sides by sofas draped in moth-eaten cashmere throws.

At the end of the drawing room, a covered balcony gave onto the street. The Baron emerged from its shelter, his faded blond hair combed back, pinstripe suit a little tight, a pink square of kerchief poking jauntily from his breast pocket. He glided between the antique furniture, one arm behind his back, with the rictus grin of a man well used to meeting and greeting. The only element detracting from the statesmanlike bearing was the geriatric Maltese terrier snuffling behind, nose pressed to his ankle.

'Rufus Sanguinetti,' he said. 'What's it been? Ten years?'

'Seventeen.'

Rufus stiffened slightly as the Baron shook his hand. Even with his father's stoop, their height difference was less than expected: Spike glanced down and saw stacked leather heels on the Baron's brogues.

The Maltese terrier switched attention to Rufus's trouser leg. 'She can smell something,' the Baron said.

Rufus glanced down as well. 'Must be the General.'

'The General?'

'General Ironside, our Jack Russell.'

'You have a dog now, Rufus? I didn't know.'

'Why would you?' Rufus screwed up his eyes. 'Is that a nef?'

The Baron turned. On the console table behind lay a gleaming model ship, a silver galleon with four masts. 'My great-great-grandfather was awarded it for services to the Maltese fleet.'

'A drinking vessel?'

'Ornamental. Though we do have a salt-cellar nef at our hunting lodge in Wardija. That said, if you detach the nautilus shell . . .' The Baron turned and headed back across the drawing room, Rufus following slowly behind, dog still attached to his leg.

The Baroness placed a hand on Spike's shoulder. 'Poor Rufus,' she whispered. 'After what happened to your mother. And now David . . .' She inhaled suddenly through yellowing teeth. 'A drink?'

'Allow me.'

The decanters on the drinks trolley were strung with tarnished silver name tags. On the lower shelf squatted a phalanx of ancient-looking mixers. 'I take a vodka and ice,' the Baroness said. 'A Scotch and dry for Michael.'

The icebox exuded the aroma of stale freezers.

'Please,' the Baroness said. 'Your father first. I forget: what is his tipple?'

'Just fizzy water these days.' Spike instantly regretted the suggestion, seeing that there was none. 'I'll give him some tonic. He'll never notice.'

'Standards, darlink,' the Baroness chided. 'Come. We find some in the cellar.'

3

They descended the palazzo through rooms of dust-sheeted furniture and unintelligible, bleached-out tapestries. On the occasional exposed table, amid the tea caddies and potpourri, sat photo frames of the Baron and his wife, posing with international dignitaries of another era: minor British royals, ageing French rock stars, a suited Asian who might once have been the Prime Minister of Japan. The absence of family portraits was a reminder to Spike that – like the Mifsuds – the Baron and Baroness were childless.

The kitchen lay in the basement, small barred windows high in its walls, like a prison cell, Spike thought. A wooden ceiling fan hung motionless, while open on the Formica table was a Maltese newspaper: evidently the kitchen was Clara the maid's domain.

'This way.'

The Baroness was beckoning to Spike from the open doorway. Within, a broad stone staircase curved downwards. The steps were worn with footmarks, their pallor a reminder that Malta was formed of the same limestone as a certain British-forged fortress at the mouth of the Mediterranean. What was it about Empire-builders and malleable rock? Places in which to carve their own image?

The temperature fell. '*Eccoci*,' the Baroness murmured, falling for some reason into Italian. She flipped on a stuttering light to reveal a cellar lined with wine racks, most of them empty. 'You used to like it down here as a boy,' she said. 'You remember? When you visited with David and Teresa. You said it reminded you of St Michael's Cave in Gibraltar.'

A drop of murky water fell onto the Baroness's hair, melting into the sand-coloured strands. 'San Pellegrino in the corner. We bring up four, *da*?'

Spike crouched beneath the vaulted roof towards the racks. Carved into the walls, a foot or so above the floor, was a line of small crucifixes.

'They date from the Second World War,' the Baroness said, seeing Spike looking. 'The Malaspinas opened their cellars as an air-raid shelter. Hundreds of people sleeping on the floor each night. They used to carve crosses above their camp beds to keep themselves safe.'

Spike slid out the first two bottles, their labels slick and loose.

'A charitable family,' the Baroness said, 'even then.' She held out an elegantly wrinkled hand. 'Come. We go back up.'

4

Rufus and the Baron sat on the covered balcony, rocking in their chairs like a couple of Mississippi landowners out on their porches. As Spike approached, he heard Rufus saying, 'But he'd had business meetings scheduled, he'd been in Gozo . . .'

'Gozo?'

'Visiting a church, I believe. No thanks, son, not thirsty. Which church was it David went to in Gozo?'

'Our Lady of St Agatha.'

'Our Lady of St Agatha,' Rufus repeated, 'and at 10 a.m. on a Monday, which sounds like work to me, so hardly the conduct of someone about to –'

Spike cleared his throat. 'I think we're sitting down.'

As soon as the Baron began to move, Rufus clambered to his feet. 'Michael's offered to help with the wake.'

'That's very kind,' Spike said to the Baron as he passed.

'The least I can do.'

'Gentlemen?' came the Baroness's soprano voice.

The dining room gave onto another side of the courtyard. Four places had been laid at the end of a long, cherrywood table. Between them sat a decanter of red wine and a tureen heated by tea lights.

'Rufus?' the Baroness said, drawing out a chair at the head.

Above, flickering in the candlelight, hung a more recent portrait of the Baron. He stood somewhat awkwardly, arms concealed by black robes. Stitched to the front of his garment was a white, eight-pointed Maltese cross.

The Baroness followed Rufus's gaze. 'Somewhat vulgar, but we do have a duty to support our local artists.'

Rufus sat down. 'When did you join the order?' he said, looking at the Baron.

'Last year.'

'And about time too,' the Baroness added, reaching over to the tureen, 'given how much charitable work Michael does. Not to mention the business he has brought to these islands, at no personal benefit to himself.'

As if in confirmation of this, she raised the lid to reveal a humble dish of baked pasta. 'Clara's speciality,' she said, spooning some steaming penne onto Rufus's plate. 'She's more an Italian Maltese than a British.'

Silence weighed on the table.

'So you're a knight, then?' Spike said.

The Baron smiled modestly. 'Only in the modern sense.'

'Which is?'

The Baron did not need to be asked twice. 'To understand the modern,' he said in the tones of the practised after-dinner speaker, 'first we must return to the past.' He launched into an indulgent history of the Order of St John, 'the oldest chivalric order in the world' – its origin as a pilgrims' hospital in Jerusalem in 1099, its militarisation during the Crusades, its eviction from the Holy Land after the fall of Jerusalem, a stint on Rhodes before finally being awarded Malta in 1530. This had been a gift from the Spanish Emperor, Charles V, after the knights' earlier struggles against the infidel, granted at a rent of two Maltese hunting falcons a year, one for the Viceroy of Sicily, one for the Emperor himself. 'A prescient move,' the Baron said proudly, 'as of course the knights went on to win the Great Siege of 1565, so repelling the Ottomans and saving the whole of Christendom from Islamic domination.'

Rufus gave a snort. 'Saviours of Christendom in 1565. Of Europe in World War II –'

'So what exactly is a knight?' Spike said, cutting him off.

The Baron looked sharply at Rufus, then resumed. 'The Knights of St John were chosen from the great Catholic families of Europe. There were three hundred or so living on Malta at any one time, and they clustered together according to their nationalities, or "langues" – French, German, English, Spanish, Italian, et cetera. Each nationality had its own "auberge", or inn, from where they administered the islands – the Italians took care of shipping, the French the hospital, and so on. A bit like an early European Commission, I always say.'

I'll bet you do, Spike thought.

'By the time Napoleon captured Malta in 1798,' the Baron went on, 'the knights had grown decadent. The gunpowder they'd stored against future Turkish attacks had become rotten. The strength of Europe had increased, so their role as protectors of the Catholic Church was no longer relevant. They put up minimal resistance, and were expelled, after which the British were forced to free Malta from French tyranny, so giving us our 150 happy years as part of the British Empire, before independence arrived in 1964.'

'So the knights vanished?' Spike said.

'Not exactly. They no longer had a home, so they splintered. The British and German "langues" grew to accommodate Protestantism. The Italians retrenched to Rome. And that was when we started to look to the old traditions.'

Rufus glanced up from his penne. 'The St John Ambulance. Finest volunteer brigade in the world.'

'That was the principal contribution of the British "langue", yes.'

Spike had seen the ambulances without ever associating them with knights and sieges. 'We have them in Gib.'

'Indeed . . . the naval bases of Gibraltar and Malta were among the first parts of Empire to receive the service.'

'In 1883,' Rufus said.

'But don't forget the work of the other chapters,' the Baron said quickly. 'The German "langue" still runs hospitals and nursing homes, despite being persecuted by the Nazis on account of their Christian faith. The Sovereign Order in Rome now organises up to 100,000 volunteers in over 120 countries. We even have a hospital in Jerusalem, within sight of the original hospital the order founded nine centuries ago. And, to complete the circle, the order now has significant holdings in Malta, with a number of the annual dinners and events held here in Valletta.'

'It is particularly appropriate Michael has been invited to join,' the Baroness said, 'given that members of his family were knights by birth, before the order even came to Malta.'

'Does Teresa's charity form part of your work?' Spike said.

The Baron wiped his mouth with a napkin thoughtfully. 'Whilst we respect the concept of Teresa's charity, we, like many others on the island, consider it . . . misguided.'

'*Custos pauperum*,' Rufus said.

Spike assumed his father was just speaking with his mouth full, but the phrase seemed to have an effect on the Baron. 'That's easy for you to say, Rufus – you don't have to live here.'

Spike looked from one to the other, as though preparing to arbitrate a legal mediation.

'The Grand Master of the Knights still bears the title "*Custos Pauperum*", Rufus explained. ' "Guardian of the Poor". For the original Knights of St John, the poor didn't just represent Christ. They *were* Christ. The hospital in Jerusalem looked after the needy regardless of creed or colour.'

'And so they should be looked after,' the Baron said, 'just not here in Malta. We're already the most densely populated country in the EU. Put together, our islands are smaller than the Isle of Wight. There's simply not enough room for a continuous influx of migrants.'

'I assure you,' Rufus said, 'that for a Gibraltarian, Malta is positively spacious.'

Spike glanced back up at the portrait. The ancient monastic outfit in the contemporary style appeared faintly ridiculous.

'We clear ourself,' the Baroness said, 'it is good for us.'

The Baron remained seated, arms crossed, as Spike gathered the plates. 'I visited the cathedral today,' he said. 'The Caravaggios were magnificent.'

'Special, special paintings,' the Baroness murmured, carrying the tureen to the sideboard.

The Baron was shaking his head. 'The Co-Cathedral packed out with cattle no doubt, all pointing their camera phones. One thousand years of heritage reduced by the Maltese government to a circus.'

'*Custos pauperum*,' Rufus repeated, and this time the Baron threw down his napkin and returned to the drawing room.

'*Digestif?*' the Baroness asked.

Spike stared across the table at Rufus. 'We should probably –'

'Please excuse Michael,' the Baroness said quietly. 'He is still shaken by what happened to David and Teresa. It was he who had to make the identification. *In situ*, as it were.'

The Maltese terrier limped into the dining room, the Baroness scooping it into her arms, pressing its shaggy white coat to her bosom. Beneath its eyes, the fur was marked with rusty stains, as though it had been weeping blood. 'Your master and David were very close lately, weren't they?' the Baroness chimed in a sing-song voice as she caressed the dog's muzzle.

Goodbyes said, Spike escorted Rufus through the dark streets, passing a silent group of nuns coming the other way. He checked his mobile and found a spinning message icon in the corner: Zahra, confirming the trip tomorrow. His spirits lifted momentarily, then he remembered his bruised elbow and accompanying warning. *Go home, foreigner.*

✳

Father de Maro brings the Fiat to a halt in the scrubby car park behind the chapel. He opens its dented door, straining against the breeze. What is that saying the Italians have? *Febbraio, febbraietto*, short and cursed. How accurate, he thinks to himself as he battles his way out of the driver's seat.

His cassock billows as he opens the back door and takes out

two plastic bags. One contains candles, the other the loaves of bread he picked up from the bakery on his way through Rabat. Only two trades left in Gozo that get a man up before dawn: God and dough. Head down against the breeze, the priest sets off towards the chapel.

As he walks, he thinks to himself – as he does each year – of the absurdity of tonight's ceremony. The Blessing of the Loaves ... The earliest images of St Agatha showed her tilting up a tray towards God. Medieval monks had assumed that what lay on the tray was bread: two indeterminate brown lumps. Nowadays, Malta's patron saint is better known to be holding up her own breasts, sliced off on the orders of a spurned and lascivious Roman governor.

The innocence of those monks ... Most of the religious art the priest has seen is unstinting in its violence. Is the gore a way of showing people the dedication demanded of them by their faith? Or is there something else at play? Titillation? Or a warning that with beauty – for the saints were always beautiful – comes danger, so be satisfied with your lot, you plain and humble folk, and get back to work.

Clumps of prickly pears sprout from the limestone that surrounds the chapel, last year's purple fruits withered on the spongy rims of their pads. As the priest rounds the corner, he pauses to stare out over the cliff face. The channel between Gozo and Comino is a fury of blue and white flecks. Waves crash into the caves below. These days, the priest is aware of how he takes refuge in the mechanics of the job, finds irony in its ancient absurdities. But a view like this ... He breathes in the salty air, then turns towards the chapel with renewed purpose.

Entering the vestibule, he glances up at the madonna above the lintel, her placid eyes staring out to sea. As he looks back down, he stops. A dusty black motorcycle is parked to the side of the chapel.

The priest remembers the art historian who promised to return before feast day. He hadn't imagined him on a motorbike, but then on the rare occasions he does make it over to the main island, he is amazed at how society is changing. Sometimes you barely see a Maltese face.

He expects to find the historian sitting inside on the bench seat, but no one is there. The door to the chapel is ajar. Had he forgotten to lock it last night? More than likely.

Putting down the heavier of the two bags, he extends a hand to the latch, hesitating as he sees a chunk of wood chiselled from beneath the lock. Someone must have broken in. Judging by the motorbike, they are still inside.

As the priest steps backwards, he stumbles on the candles and knocks against the bench seat. A clatter comes from inside the door, and he turns and hurries back out to the path.

Father de Maro's wheezing breaths dissipate in the breeze. Footsteps approach, crunching on shingle. He stares out again at the majesty of the sea, then turns to face his fate.

Chapter Five

Spike finished the portion of deep-fried dates and patted his stomach. Time to find something green to eat on this island. Moving to the edge of the walkway, he looked down into the St James Ditch, noting that the builders' skip in which Mifsud's photographs had landed had vanished, only a pale rectangle remaining on the muddy ground. When he glanced back up, Zahra was making her approach beneath the City Gate.

Zahra's blue cotton dress stopped just below the knee, revealing smooth tanned calves and small feet in spotless white trainers. A row of mother-of-pearl buttons followed her neckline downwards; in deference to winter, a cream cardigan was looped across her shoulders.

Spike waved at her, his fingers still covered in a sugary sheen from breakfast. Zahra continued towards him, face neutral. As they kissed hello, he caught a hint of the citrus scent he'd once known well. 'I thought you'd be coming from the other direction,' he said.

'I dropped by the office first.'

'But you're free now?'

She nodded, a strand of black hair falling from behind one ear. Spike quashed the urge to tuck it back, then followed her onto the number 45 bus. He hovered in the aisle; eventually she lifted her handbag from the seat beside her, and he sat down. A vintage Penguin paperback nestled inside. 'What are you reading?'

'*The Great Gatsby.*'

'Any good?'

'Yes.'

'Great?'

She conceded a tight smile, then looked away as a pair of elderly men boarded, one carrying a pilgrim's wooden staff.

'So,' Spike said to Zahra's cool profile.

She turned, and he stared into her almond-shaped eyes. 'So,' she replied.

'I'm sorry about last time. There was a lot going on.'

'Why did you ask me to come to Gozo, Spike?'

The bus pulled out, and Spike glanced again at the pilgrims. The taller man was resting his head on the shoulder of the smaller. Spike took out the Mifsud diary and handed it to Zahra, open on today's date.

'Olsa,' she read aloud.

'This belonged to David.'

Zahra scoffed. 'So now it is David who was having the affair. With some Russian beauty called Olsa.'

Spike flipped back to the week before Mifsud's death.

'Our Lady of St Agatha,' Zahra said slowly, her reading more tentative than her spoken English. 'O-L-S-A . . . I get it.'

'I think David may have been working on something in this church. Unconnected to his day job.'

'So?'

Spike closed the diary. 'So I haven't told you everything.'

'Imagine that.'

The bus came to a halt, and a Maltese youth got on. He leered unashamedly at Zahra; Spike wondered if he'd have done so had she not been dressed as a European. When he glared back, the youth dropped his gaze and fell into a seat behind the pilgrims.

'The police are convinced it was a murder–suicide,' Spike resumed. 'But I don't buy it. That level of violence, to a woman he loved . . .' He winced as a photograph of the murder scene flickered through his mind. 'Yesterday I went to the police station in Floriana. I spoke to Assistant Commissioner Azzopardi. Have you heard of him?'

'His father's the Commissioner.'

'He told me Teresa had sex with someone shortly before she died.'

'So she *was* having an affair?'

Spike lowered his voice. 'According to the forensic evidence.'

'Which you don't believe.'

'I just can't see my uncle committing murder. Can you?'

Zahra shook her head.

'My father feels the same, so I promised him I'd look into it. Retrace David's movements in the days leading up to his death. So far so uneventful, but then things start to get strange. I find out David was in Gozo the week before he died – and that he had appointments scheduled for the day *after* he was supposed to have committed suicide. Then, when I pick up some photos he'd taken, some psycho tries to push me into the ditch by the bus terminus.'

'What photos?'

Spike glanced over. 'I'm fine. Thanks for asking.'

Zahra bit back a smile.

'They're of a painting.'

'What does Gozo have to do with it?'

'I don't know yet. But there was something there that David was interested in.'

Zahra paused. 'And why do you want me?'

'You speak Maltese. I thought it might come in handy.'

She folded her arms across her cardigan. 'I knew it. Well, maybe you can do something for me.'

'Such as?'

'Help me find that missing girl.'

'Dinah?'

'She never registered at the family camp. Gave birth last month at the Mater Dei Hospital, then checked out and hasn't been seen since.'

'You said the migrants often disappear.'

'With a newborn?'

'What does John think?'

'He wasn't at the office this morning.'

'And what do you want me to do about it?'

Zahra narrowed her eyes and turned to the window. Spike followed her gaze. The bus was passing through the tightly bound streets of a town. To the right rose an enormous church, circular in shape like the Coliseum.

'That's the Rotunda,' Zahra said, adjusting her position to get a better view. 'You've heard of the Miracle of Mosta?'

Spike shook his head, feeling a pang as he remembered how she used to humble him with her eagerness to keep learning more.

'In World War II,' she went on, 'a German bomb fell through the roof. Hundreds of people were gathered inside for Mass. The bomb hit the floor. The people stared at it. It never exploded.'

'The power of prayer,' Spike said as the bus pulled into a rare stretch of open countryside. Most of Malta seemed determined to merge into a single urban agglomeration, but here the hills were undeveloped, their flat planed-off aspect suggesting glaciers or volcanoes. Spike remembered talk of prehistoric temples hidden deep below the ground. The concrete sprawl recommenced as they came into St Paul's Bay. 'See out there,' Zahra said.

Spike looked beyond the harbour to three wave-lashed outcrops of rock.

'That's where St Paul was shipwrecked. He was on his way to Italy but got blown off course.'

'A familiar tale.'

'The locals took him in. He converted Publius, the Roman governor, and the rest of Malta followed. One of the oldest

Christian nations in the world, and guess what their word for God is?'

'Tourism?'

'*Alla*. The only language in the world with an Arabic grammar and a Western script. Did you know that?'

'I did not.'

The pilgrims got off the bus, the younger helping the elder down the steps. The next development offered something of a party street. A hand-painted banner read 'Aaron Elvis, Tribute to the King, Every Friday'.

'Remind you of anywhere?' Zahra asked. 'What was that square in Gibraltar? Casemate?'

'Casemates,' Spike said. 'Casemates Square.'

She pointed to another deserted-looking island. 'That's Comino. Named after the cumin they used to grow.'

Spike felt another stir of sadness at the thought of Zahra exploring Malta alone. Or worse, with someone else. At last they turned into a car park and he caught a first glimpse of Gozo, rising in the distance from the choppy water.

2

The ferry lurched on the cold February sea. Ahead lay Gozo, like a brown stick on the horizon. 'Looks like a prison island,' Spike said.

Zahra was resting her forearms on the balustrade, staring out like a ship's figurehead. 'It was, in a sense. Remember Calypso?'

'Is that a bar?'

Zahra gave a stiff smile. 'A nymph.'

Spike scoured his Ancient History GCSE and came up all but empty. 'She was bad news, I seem to recall.'

'From a male perspective. She seduced Odysseus. He was meant to be sailing home to his true love but he met Calypso and became so infatuated that he lost his way. Spent seven years holed up in her cave eating sweetmeats before Zeus ordered her to release him.'

'And this was where she lived?'

'So they say.'

Spike stared out at the island. Another cathedral dome rose against the hazy sky. 'So the only way off Gozo is with the gods' help.'

'Not always. In 1551, Ottoman pirates kidnapped the whole population. Six thousand men, women and children, all sold into slavery in Africa.'

'What did the Maltese do?'

'Panicked. Dug ditches. Built forts. Laid escape tunnels under their houses. A few years later, the Great Siege took place. Which they very nearly lost.'

To the right, a dark webbed circle hung in the water. 'Is that a fish farm?'

'Tuna pens. The Maltese net them out at sea, then fatten them up here. Then they're flown to Japan for sushi. It's big money. Last year a migrant boat capsized, and the passengers grabbed onto a passing net. The trawler kept going. The catch was worth a million euros so they refused to stop.'

'Got their priorities in order.'

Some Italian tourists leaning on the railings beside them deemed the spray too much and went below deck. Patches of Zahra's cotton dress were navy with seawater.

'You've really got your bearings, Zahra.'

'John was keen to show me round, so . . .'

'Do you like it here?'

'The teaching's tough, but at least it's useful. I enjoy the court work, but it's only two days a week.'

'All migrant cases?'

'Any time they need an Arabic translator. It pays for board and lodging. David and Teresa helped me to find a room. They were so kind.'

'In a flat?'

'With a Chinese student.'

A larger wave crashed against the stern, throwing Zahra against Spike's flank. She smiled as she regained her balance, then pushed the damp hair back from her face. On her wrist, Spike saw a heavy diver's watch. 'Do you miss Morocco?' he said.

Her lips grew tight. 'I try not to think about home.'

The tannoy requested drivers to return to their vehicles. As the ferry closed in on Mġarr Harbour, Spike looked out at the limestone cliffs. All along this side of the island, they were pockmarked with dark, slurping caves.

3

The ferry terminal looked as though it had enjoyed a recent injection of EU funds. The automatic doors parted sleekly to a freshly tarmacked road lined with white Mercedes cabs. On closer inspection, the taxis were all empty, the drivers taking coffee at a pavement café.

The Italians from the boat were mid-negotiation. As Spike set off towards them, one driver sprang to his feet and met him halfway.

'Where you wanna go?' he asked, his English better than that of most Gibraltarian cabbies. He peered over at Zahra, who was bending down, dress tautening across her haunches as she knelt to do up a shoelace.

'St Agatha's Church.'

'Which one?'

Zahra straightened up. 'Hello, lady,' the driver called over. She threw him a look, and he turned back to Spike, briefly chastened. 'We've got 365 churches on Malta and Gozo. One for each day of the year. There's a few dedicated to Agatha; she's our patron saint.'

'Our Lady of St Agatha?'

'I take you to the chapel, then.' He shouted at the other drivers, who were still negotiating, then opened his cab.

Spike and Zahra got in the back, the driver shunting his seat forward to make room for Spike's long legs as they climbed the hills above the port. 'Where you from, lady?' he called behind, eyes feeding on Zahra in the rear-view mirror. She said something quietly in Maltese, and his eyes returned to the road.

'So this is Gozo,' Zahra said to Spike.

It felt like a more rustic version of Malta. Roadside taverns wore blackboards offering varieties of rabbit: stewed, potted, roasted.

'How many Gozoites are there?'

'Gozitans. Thirty thousand.'

'Same as Gibraltar.'

'But ten times the size.'

They turned onto a clifftop road through villages of decrepit sandstone. Less tourism: less money. A farmer in dungarees crouched in a field, smoking as he checked his cold frames.

'I think that must be the Blue Lagoon,' Zahra said, pointing through the window to an inlet bisecting the island of Comino. The pale sand that had accumulated in the calmer currents lent the water an azure glow. 'In summer it's full of yachts. Amazing scuba.'

'Is that why John gave you that watch?'

There was a pause. 'I haven't taken my test yet. Why don't you wear a watch, by the way?'

'Makes me feel restricted.'

'Of course it does.'

A bus passed on the other side of the road. Dull and grey: the Arriva fleet had made it to Gozo.

'You here for the *festa*?' the driver yelled back.

'*Festa*?' Spike repeated.

'Feast Day of St Agatha. The Blessing of the Loaves.'

Zahra glanced over. Was that why David had arranged to visit Gozo today?

They turned down a track towards the clifftop. A single vehicle was parked ahead in a dusty piece of wasteland. Beyond rose the pale limestone of a chapel, its tower crowned by a white cross.

'That's Father de Maro's car,' the driver said as they came to a halt. 'He's getting on a bit, but if you talk loudly enough, he'll give you a history of the church.'

'Can you wait for us here?' Spike asked.

'I've got a booking in Rabat. I can be back in half an hour?'

Spike paid up.

'Check out the graffiti on the chapel wall,' the driver called through his window. 'Knights did that centuries back.' He drove away, leaving them standing in the breeze by Father de Maro's rusty Fiat.

4

The Fiat had dents in the bodywork from what looked like a series of minor prangs. A sticker on the windscreen read 'Gozo Curia'. On the dashboard lay a half-eaten tube of Polos.

Spike walked with Zahra towards the rear of the chapel. Jagged limestone surrounded its walls, cacti sprouting from the crags.

'Have you tried any *bajtra*?' Zahra said.

'Any what?'

'It's a prickly-pear liqueur. Not bad, actually. The knights invented it.'

'Alcoholic?'

Zahra raised her eyes defiantly. 'I'm not feeling so religious these days.'

The chapel's small barred windows were clogged with sparrows' nests. Carved into the limestone was an image of a sailing boat, with an inscription below.

'*Non gode l'immunità ecclesiastica*,' Spike read aloud. 'That'll be the knights' graffiti.'

'What does it mean?'

'That this chapel refuses sanctuary to criminals.'

'Is it Latin?'

'Italian, I think.'

They stopped at the clifftop. The Mediterranean's oily gleam suggested winter's chill still lurked beneath. Beyond, Spike saw the entrance to the Blue Lagoon marked by a row of sharp triangular rocks.

A herring gull took off from the cliff edge, a lump of something brown left below. 'Father de Maro must be a bit of a twitcher,' Spike said, pointing at the remains of a loaf of bread.

Zahra was already walking towards the chapel. Spike watched the gull circle above in the updraughts, then accelerated his pace to catch her up.

5

Set above the pediment of the chapel was a bas-relief of the madonna. 'There's a tradition in Malta,' Zahra said. 'Whichever way the eyes of the madonna point is where the knights have buried their treasure.'

Spike followed the madonna's gaze to see the herring gull swooping back down over the edge of the cliff. 'A half-eaten chunk of bird food,' he said aloud, but Zahra had already gone inside.

A loose carrier bag lay in the vestibule; littering the floor were a number of broken white candles. Zahra moved to the main door; it was pushed to, the metal tongue of a lock sticking out from the frame.

Spike followed Zahra inside, the aroma immediately transporting him back home, to Sundays accompanying his mother to Gibraltar's Catholic cathedral for interminable morning services. The smell had been the only aspect he'd liked – musty prayer books infused with incense. He thought of the gymnasium reek of the oratory and wondered if the Baron hadn't had a point when he'd accused the Maltese government of selling out the knights' heritage.

The interior was small and plain, just a stone aisle with two banks of plastic chairs on either side, the altar a mere table on a stage. What light there was came from the small barred windows.

'Hello?' Spike called out.

A doorway lay to the side of the altar. 'Maybe he's in the . . .'

'Vestry,' Spike completed, deciding his churchgoing childhood had not been entirely wasted. He surveyed the walls. A clumsily painted Annunciation, a chocolate-box manger scene. The only decent piece was a Maltese cross in the corner, intricately carved.

Spike lifted his eyes above the main door. Room enough for a painting, but the space was empty. Outlined on the plaster was a faint oval shape, as though something had been recently removed.

'Locked,' Zahra called out, drawing her cardigan across her chest.

Spike was still taking in the ghostly shape on the plaster.

'Come on, Spike. It's cold. The priest's not here.'

He turned and followed her back into the vestibule. As he started to close the door, he paused. Etched into the jamb was a rectangular outline, as though a chunk of wood had been cut out, then glued back in. He tried to press down the metal lock but it was fixed. He pushed the door to, then stepped onto the path.

The gull was back on the clifftop, pecking at the loaf of bread. Zahra clapped and it flew away. Three more gulls emerged from below, circling on the squalling wind.

Spike glanced back at the madonna, then followed her eyes towards the cliffs.

'What is it now?' Zahra said.

The wind buffeted Spike's jumper. Waves crashed out of sight. As he neared the rocky edge, he dropped to his knees. Another gull appeared, swooping up on the currents that were rising from the base of the cliffs. Spike might have thought he was closing in on a nesting colony, except he knew that herring gulls nested in May. *Febbraio, febbraietto*, he said to himself as he crawled closer.

'Be careful,' he heard behind.

The limestone powdered the knees of his jeans. One of the gulls made as if to dive-bomb him, defecating into the drop in front. Two outcrops rose on the edge; using them as handgrips, Spike inched his head outwards, strands of dark hair blowing into his eyes. Five metres below, a crag stuck out from the cliff face. Draped over it was a long black figure. A gull was perched at the head, wings arched.

Spike shouted down but his voice was muted by the breeze. Was this some religious effigy, discarded after a previous feast day? As he leaned out further, his hand crumbled off a piece of rock, which rolled down the cliff face, alarming the gull, which squawked raucously as it wafted away.

A face stared upwards. Two red, emptied holes were all that remained of the eyes.

Spike scrambled backwards, elbows scraping the limestone, to find Zahra still standing on the cliff edge. As he got to his feet, he saw a man moving behind her.

'*What?*' Zahra said impatiently.

Spike brushed the dust from his clothes. The taxi driver was walking towards them.

'Not good,' Spike said. 'Not good at all.'

6

'Fancy a coffee?' Azzopardi said.

'No thank you.'

After calling a drinks order into the lobby, Azzopardi came back into the interview room. He wore the same navy Armani suit as in the Depot, though newly pressed. 'The head of the Gozo police,' he murmured, shaking his head as he sat down opposite Spike at the table. 'The smallest incident and he calls me.' He leaned in conspiratorially. 'I heard a phrase the other day – "If he fell into a bucket of tits, he'd come up sucking his own thumb." ' Azzopardi smiled; Spike didn't smile back.

'So let's go over this again,' Azzopardi said, clicking on the tape recorder. 'You read in your uncle's diary that he had a meeting scheduled with Father de Maro. You and your friend are curious, and decide to keep the appointment, wondering if perhaps he'd been using the Father as a confessor for his marital problems. Then you find the priest's body stuck halfway down a cliff face.'

'That's about it.'

'How did you know the body was there?'

'I saw gulls circling.'

'So you peered down.'

'Correct.'

'The taxi driver, Mr Fenech – he says he saw you climbing back up. As though you might have pushed the priest off yourself.'

'Why don't you examine the chapel door, Mr Azzopardi? Someone broke in.'

'You?'

Spike spoke quietly, trying to curb his frustration. 'The priest's eyes had been pecked out. Herring gulls may be fast workers, but they're not that hungry. You've already seen our ferry tickets; we'd only been in Gozo an hour.' He glanced up at the wall clock. 'Make that six now.'

Azzopardi's sleeve lifted as he clicked off the tape, revealing his striped friendship bracelet, souvenir of some music festival or backpacking trip. 'My Mobile Squad ran a check on you after you left the Depot,' he said. 'Law school in London, paid for by the Gibraltar government. Recipient of a Denning Scholarship, yet still you end up back in Gibraltar working for some no-name local firm.' He smiled. 'Nothing interesting until last summer, when you hit the headlines with a case in Morocco. What was it the press called you – the Devil's Advocate? Five people dead?'

'I protect my clients, Mr Azzopardi. Sometimes people don't like it.'

'A client who's currently languishing in a Moroccan jail.'

'I completed my brief. Mr Hassan now has new defence counsel.'

Azzopardi stood and moved to Spike's side of the table. 'Listen,' he said, 'I know this is tough for you and your family. But sometimes when you stare too hard at something, you start to see things that aren't there.'

'I'm pretty sure the priest's body was there.'

Azzopardi clicked the machine back on. 'Tell me about the girl.'

'We met last year in Morocco. I helped her secure a visa for Gibraltar. She wanted to move somewhere bigger so I found her a job in Malta with my aunt.'

'She's lucky to have her own personal counsel.'

'I doubt she would agree.'

'She's a migrant, right?'

'A court interpreter. Working for a wage, same as you. The only difference is her father didn't get her the job.'

Azzopardi stared down coldly. For the first time, his youthfulness took on a menacing quality, like a child plucking the wings from an insect. 'Get that Moroccan back in here,' he said. 'And don't make any plans to leave Valletta.'

Spike was already on his way to the door.

7

A blue stained-glass lamp protruded from the portico of Victoria Police Station. For a country so proud of independence, Malta seemed to have difficulty throwing off its British roots. At least Gibraltar admitted its colonial status ... Spike sat down on the steps beneath, mobile phone in hand. 'Room 201,' he said once the receptionist had picked up. Twelve more rings, then, 'Hello?'

'Dad?'

'Son! How are you?'

'Fine ...' Spike said, ill at ease at his father's good spirits. 'But I'm not going to be back till late.'

'What are you up to?'

'With an old friend. We're checking out Gozo.'

'Good for you. Take your mind off things.'

'You OK?'

'Been out and about with the Baron. We've booked a venue for the wake, fabulous little bistro in Valletta, rabbit a speciality.'

'What is it with rabbit here?'

'It's the national dish. The knights banned the locals from hunting. Eating rabbit was a sign of rebellion.' Rufus paused to take a bite of something himself. 'You know, I think we may have misjudged the Baron. He's been most helpful.'

'He does seem to have been genuinely fond of Uncle David.'

'Lord alone knows why. Anyway, you enjoy yourself. Don't worry about me.'

Spike hung up, watching the city's high street rumble sleepily by. Gozitans seemed to refer to their capital as 'Rabat', preferring the old Arabic name to the more colonial 'Victoria'. Yet more identity confusion . . . He made a second call.

'M'learned friend.'

'Hi, Jess. How are you?'

'Fine, though I seem to be seeing more of your dog than my fiancé. How's Malta?'

'Bit grim.'

'When are you back?'

'The funerals are tomorrow. We'll be home the following afternoon.'

'Relieved to hear it.'

'Why?'

'Hamish has landed a new job. Heard of Caledonian Capital?'

'No.'

'Nor had I. But apparently it's tremendously exciting. He has to relocate to London so we've moved the wedding forward.'

'London?'

'I've been looking into a transfer to the Met.'

Spike grimaced. 'Sounds tremendously exciting.'

'Ha ha. Anyway, we're following in the footsteps of John and Yoko. And Sean Connery.'

'The Gibraltar quickie marriage? Don't forget Mark Thatcher.'

'I've been trying to. We'd love to have you as a witness.'

'It'd be an honour.'

'*Tenkiu*, Spike.'

He glanced round: Zahra was coming down the steps of the police station. 'Got to go,' he said.

'Someone more interesting?'

'I'll call you back.'

He got to his feet as Zahra shook her head wearily. 'They're typing up my statement. Did you have to give fingerprints?'

'And a DNA swab.'

'Christ.'

Spike turned to see a motorbike cruising along the road. The driver wore a black helmet. It slowed by the police station, then revved away.

8

The ferry to Malta was empty save for a few melancholy lorry drivers staring into space. Zahra took a table on the lower deck as Spike paced the gunwale outside, profiting from a brief inclination to make phone calls.

Galliano was at the office; he confirmed that the cocaine-smuggling case was as good as dead. At least Harrington had paid all fees and expenses. 'Unlike that Hamish fellow. He hasn't even returned my calls. The pipeline's looking a bit thin, Spike.'

'I'll be back at work next week.'

'I've heard that one before.'

Next came Drew Stanford-Trench. The background hum made Spike yearn for a moment to be home in Gib. 'Spikey . . .' Stanford-Trench began, before remembering the nature of Spike's trip and retreating to a quieter corner of whichever pub he was in. They talked for a while about the drug-smuggling case, able to speak freely now that the trial had collapsed.

'So you really think Harrington was talking Serbian?' Stanford-Trench said.

'Sounded like it.'

'I didn't think he had it in him; he seemed so . . . dull.'

'And were you close to tracking down the owner of *The Restless Wave*?'

'Ish. I subscribed to a website called Yachtfinder which listed the name of the holding company for the boat. The address given was a PO box in Belgrade. The surname Radovic had been taken from a stolen passport. Then the trail went cold.'

'Well, whoever Radovic is, I'll bet you he's had dealings with Harrington's asset management company.'

'Maybe, Spike. Anyway, remember that English girl I met?'

'It's hard to keep up.'

'The one I took to the Tunnel. She's coming back to Gib next month. And guess what? She's bringing a friend.'

Spike heard Stanford-Trench call out, 'Same again . . . actually, with a top,' then resume: 'I've just seen a photo. Long legs, dark hair, in need of a bit of rescuing. Right up your *strasse*, I'd say.'

Spike ended the call and went back inside.

9

Zahra raised her dark glassy eyes. 'Sorry. It's just . . . finding the body. Brought back a few memories.'

'I'll get you a drink.'

The ferry bar wasn't serving alcohol so Spike zigzagged back with two cups of tea.

'Thank you,' Zahra said as she pulled off the plastic lid. She blew on her drink, eyes on the misty perspex windows of the ferry. 'You know what some of the migrants do?' she said. 'Before they get picked up?'

'What?'

'Throw away their ID. Passports, papers. Dump their whole lives into the sea.'

Spike waited. Experience had taught him that it was wiser to let her talk it out.

'It means they can tell Maltese immigration they're from any country that suits. If Burkina Faso is at peace, they can say they're from Ivory Coast, which is at war. You follow me?'

Spike raised the weeping eyelet to his mouth.

'Of course, sometimes it's too obvious. A Somali has a certain look. Long neck, copper skin. But generally it works.'

'Sounds sensible.'

'Some of the names we get: Zinédine. Pelé. That's boys for you. The detail the women like to change is their age. A hell of a lot of eighteen-year-old girls wash up on Malta.' She raised the cup to her mouth, then put it down without drinking. 'Except Dinah. I found the records of her visa application. Dinah Kassim, thirty-four years old. Her little boy is called Saif. He'll be four weeks old now.'

'What about the father?'

'Not on the scene.'

'What's your point?'

'Dinah's visa application was turned down. She and her son were due to be repatriated to Somalia next week.'

'So they found another way to get to Italy.'

'I spoke to her friends again. They've heard nothing. No texts, no calls.'

'She's keeping her head down.'

'But she was always on her phone. Loved sending picture messages of Saif. The light of her life, she called him. Her reason for living.'

'Maybe she ditched her phone on the crossing.' Spike glanced across at the grey-green Mediterranean, wondering how Odysseus had felt when finally escaping this island. 'What was that drink you mentioned? With the prickly pears?'

'*Bajtra*.'

'Yes. We should get us some of that.'

97

Spike and Zahra sat at a table for two on the waterfront. A railing divided the restaurant from the coast road, along which the occasional fish delivery truck trundled, followed by bicycles or courting couples arm in arm. Beyond lay Marsaxlokk Harbour – *Marsa-shlock*, Zahra had pronounced it – a horseshoe-shaped inlet where a flotilla of fishing boats bobbed in the evening breeze. The boats' yellow-and-turquoise hulls were as garish as Malta's buses once had been. Painted on the side of each was an eye, almond-shaped like Zahra's, with a black pupil and open lashes on either side. Whatever the type of boat, the eye seemed to be the same size, giving them a spookily living quality, as though they all belonged to the same species at different stages of growth. Eyes of Osiris, Zahra had called them, introduced to Malta in Phoenician times to ward off evil spirits.

A fisherman on the nearest jetty rattled up his anchor chain in advance of an evening sortie. With his thick neck and swollen chest, he resembled one of the protesters Spike had seen outside the charity office. Spike looked away, then saw the owner watching them from inside the restaurant; the only other customers had left half an hour ago.

'Time for those prickly pears?' Spike said.

'It's more a *digestif*,' Zahra replied, easing a grey flake of fresh tuna onto her fork.

Spike was reminded that there were certain pleasures to dining alone. You could eat quickly, enjoy your prickly-pear juice whenever you –

'What do you want out of life?' Zahra suddenly said.

Spike looked up, apprehensive.

'If you could script it. Make it how you wanted.'

He straightened his cutlery, which the owner took as a cue to swoop. '*Grazzi*,' Zahra said in Maltese as he collected their plates. Spike assumed this would mark the end of her line of questioning, but she was still looking at him intently across the table. He sighed. 'God, I don't know, Zahra. Same as most people, I suppose. A reasonable amount of happiness. Health and well-being for friends and family. World peace. Why, what do you want?'

Zahra smiled. 'I knew you wouldn't answer properly.'

'It's not a very interesting question. You play the hand you're dealt. It's like asking what colour you want the sun to be apart from yellow.'

'The sun's a million different colours.'

'You know what I mean.'

'No,' she said, 'I don't.'

The owner returned, pad in hand. Spike raised an eyebrow, and Zahra spoke again in Maltese; a moment later the owner reappeared with an unlabelled bottle and two ice-filled tumblers. After cracking off the top, he retreated, leaving the bottle between them.

'Looks promising.'

'Same old Spike,' Zahra said. 'Get the booze in when your father's not around.'

Spike decided to ignore that. Reaching for the bottle, he felt her hand touch his, the skin as smooth and warm as he remembered. 'Uh-uh,' she said. 'You're going to have to buy a shot.'

'I was hoping to pick up the tab.'

'Not money. Answers. One answer buys you one shot.' The smile found her eyes but her tone was sharp.

'You've got to let me try some first,' he said, feeling her squeeze his knuckles. 'Check out the exchange rate.'

She took the bottle with her other hand and poured out a syrupy drop of liquid. Over the ice cubes, it changed from golden to a lurid purple. He put it to his lips: sweet cough medicine with a hint of earthiness. 'Delicious.'

'Liar.'

He waited for the burning in his oesophagus to ease. 'Potent.'

'The truth at last.'

The owner had given up on them now, cashing up at a window table with a strongbox and a bottle of Cisk beer open before him.

'Well?' Spike said. 'Fire away.'

'Same question. Your life. If you could script it.'

'Can I bring people back from the dead?' Spike asked with a throwaway laugh.

'Sadly not.'

Out to sea, fifty painted pairs of eyes stared back. 'Peter Galliano and I . . . you remember Peter? We'd structure a hedge fund in Gib which went nuclear. In return, we'd get a small percentage of the profits . . . nothing major, just enough to refurbish the house in Chicardo's and employ a full-time nurse for my dad. A governess type with a love of Italian literature who would mysteriously melt under his charm and fall in love with him.'

'So you wouldn't have to worry about him.'

'Do I get a drink for that?'

Zahra raised the bottle, then put it down. 'But what about *your* life?'

'Me?' Spike said. 'I'd buy one of those old Genoese houses on the eastern side of the Rock. Just above the beach in Catalan Bay: wrought-iron balcony, white-painted facade. Then every summer I'd pick a Mediterranean country and spend two months exploring. I'd do the occasional piece of lawyering, pro bono, just to keep my hand in.' He shrugged. 'And that would be it.'

Zahra poured out two purple fingers, which Spike gratefully knocked back. When he looked up again, he caught a flash of disappointment on her face. 'So all this happens alone?' she said.

'That's a separate question.'

She refreshed his glass, then placed her palm on the top.

'I forgot you were a stickler for the rules . . . No, not necessarily. But there's a risk if it's with someone else.'

'Why?'

She kept her hand on his glass.

'Something could go wrong. You could get . . . stuck.'

'Stuck? Interesting choice of word. What about children?'

'What about them?'

She poured out a drop more.

'The world's overcrowded enough as it is,' Spike said. 'It's hardly crying out for more Sanguinettis.' He drained his glass, then gave his head a shake, feeling his eyeballs rattle in their sockets like marbles. 'But enough of me. One drink, one question. The common market.'

Zahra let him fill up her glass; remembering she was relatively new to alcohol, he showed some restraint. 'What do you want?' he said.

She planted her elbows on the table, resting her delicate chin on her hands. 'I'd meet someone. Fall in love. Earn enough money to be comfortable. Have a baby, two maybe. Bring them up speaking English and Arabic, then, when they were old enough, take them to Morocco to see my parents' graves. That's about it.' She sipped her drink; it was unclear if the sheen in her eyes came from the booze. 'Maybe some bookshelves,' she added, smiling.

'On their own?'

She blushed. 'A house with bookshelves. And a view of the sea. Yes, that would be good.'

The owner re-emerged.

'Thank the Lord,' Spike muttered. 'Do you want me to . . .?'

'I bring machine.'

Spike topped up both glasses. Half the bottle was gone. 'Last question,' he said. 'Why did you leave Gib?'

'You've already answered that.'

'Have I?' He sensed her eyes searching his face, but could not drag his own up to meet them.

'There is hotel bar on next corner,' the owner said, proffering the Visa machine.

'We could grab another drink,' Spike suggested.

'Or a cab back to Valletta,' Zahra said, glancing down at her wristwatch as Spike tapped in his pin and paid.

11

The flat, boxy roof of the Duncan Guest House gave a vaguely North African feel. It stood in the lee of yet another church, a few yards shy of the harbourside. The terrace was closed for the night, chairs on tables; Spike held open the door for Zahra and they entered the lobby bar.

A well-oiled elderly couple sat with guidebooks and Irish coffees beneath a faded scuba-diving poster advertising the Blue Lagoon. At the desk, the receptionist checked the time, then heroically mustered a smile.

'We wondered if we could order a taxi,' Zahra said.

'They have to come from Valletta,' the receptionist replied. 'Twenty minutes.'

'Perfect,' Spike said. 'We can order a drink while we wait. Zahra?'

'Mineral water.'

'Two of those, please. And some ice.'

The receptionist glanced down at the bottle of *bajtra* in Spike's hand, then dipped into the fridge below the bar.

Zahra chose a table a few seats away from the elderly couple. Spike positioned himself beside her, placing the bottle of *bajtra* by the chair leg.

'In Malta, nothing is ever more than twenty minutes away,' Zahra said.

The couple smiled over; Spike gave a nod back, then ran a hand through his hair, feeling it already dampening in the stuffy heat of the bar. They sat for a moment in silence.

'Were you close to your uncle and aunt?' Zahra said.

'I'm sorry?'

'Teresa told me she hadn't seen you in years.'

'Jesus,' Spike muttered. 'You're really going for it tonight.'

The barman brought over a bottle of water and two glasses. When he was gone, Spike picked up the *bajtra* and poured a purple slug into each, topping up with a nominal dash of water, then taking a long slow sip. 'I suppose it was my fault, really,' he said at last. 'After my mother died, my uncle and aunt came over to Gib for the funeral. David said something to me about my dad. Suggested he was in some way responsible for her death. That he should have looked out for her more, cut off the booze, something along those lines. This from David Mifsud, who never visited, barely phoned . . .' Spike looked up. 'Enough?'

'Do you miss your mother?'

He downed his drink.

'Do you think she'd be happy with how you've turned out?'

He poured another glass. 'By the time she died she was so depressed she genuinely believed we'd be better off without her. But if she was back to her old self . . . Maybe.'

'What wouldn't she like about you?'

Spike cast his mind back. 'I think she worried I didn't take life seriously enough. Just sailed through, took the easy road, never questioned things. "You have to make *some* positive contribution to the world," she used to say, "however minor." So these days, I try and ask questions. Do the right thing.'

'Was that why you helped me in Morocco? Because it was the right thing?' Her face was fixed on his. He felt like a child again, unexpectedly berated for saying something flippant. He tried to measure his answer, then gave up. 'I felt excited when I was with you.'

'And?'

'That alarmed me.'

'Why?'

The phone was ringing at the desk. 'Taxi's coming,' the receptionist called over.

Their eyes locked. 'I think you're scared,' Zahra said. 'You don't want to take a risk because it hurts to be left.'

His voice was sharp now: 'Spare me the psychobabble, Zahra.'

The couple gestured goodnight as they picked up their guidebooks and hobbled through the inner door.

'Tell me I'm wrong,' Zahra said.

'You're wrong.'

'Why?'

'Well . . . look at you. Your mother dies in childbirth. Your father is murdered. The rest of your family never wants to see you again because you cost them their livelihoods. You've experienced more abandonment than I'll ever know. But you're not scared of opening up, or taking a risk. Bereavement doesn't close a person off. It's too simplistic.'

'You think I'm not tempted to push people away? That I don't have to make an effort to trust people?'

Spike half stood for Zahra as she headed to the Ladies, then went to reception and paid. A clatter came from the corridor, followed by the low murmur of voices. Spike followed the sound and saw Zahra crouching to pick up some guidebooks the old couple had dropped. She said something as she rose and the couple laughed. She held open the door for them to go up to their rooms; as soon as they were gone, her face fell, heavy with sadness.

'Zahra?'

She turned, and he placed his hands on her shoulders, putting his mouth to hers. At first she resisted, but then the tension seemed to drain from her body. Her lips were soft and warm.

'Your taxi . . .' came a voice. 'Oh.'

12

They lay opposite one another on their sides. The room gave onto the harbourside, street lamps gleaming through half-open curtains. The occasional passing car arced headlights over the ceiling.

Spike had the palm of one hand beneath Zahra's neck; with the other, he traced the contours of her body: shoulder blade, ribcage, hip. The smooth brown skin of her thigh and calf. On their return journey, his fingers dipped to the two small dimples he remembered above her buttocks.

She reached for his chest. He felt his groin stir again as she stroked the corrugated muscles of his stomach. 'You remember our first night in the desert?' she said.

'In the cave?'

'I wanted to be with you then.' She drew a fingertip up the dark line of hair that grew above his navel.

'I've missed you,' Spike said.

Zahra's mouth turned down a little. 'You don't have to say that.'

He edged closer to her across the mattress. 'Will you give me another chance?'

She smiled, then pulled him towards her.

13

Spike walked along the harbourfront, swinging a paper bag of pastries in one hand. The fishing boats – *luzzi*, Zahra had called them – creaked in the morning breeze. Stopping beside the jetty, he watched a fisherman and his son sorting their night-time catch into polystyrene trays. Though fresh, the fish were twisted, rigor mortis having set in as they'd suffocated in the nets. One still clung to life – a red mullet – and flipped in the tray, small mouth gaping, single yellow eye staring upwards. The father turned to Spike, a cigarette clenched between his front teeth. He gave Spike a wink, then looked away.

On the hillside behind rose the striped chimney stacks of what looked like a power station. Perhaps that was why this fishing village remained relatively undeveloped. 'Morning,' the receptionist said with a smile as Spike entered the hotel.

Spike smiled back, then bounded up the stairs to their first-floor room. Zahra was still asleep, one arm tossed on the pillow above her head like a swooning actress. Her small, tanned breasts were almost visible above the line of the sheets.

Spike closed the door carefully, but she stirred. He caught the stale but fragrant smell of lazy mornings of old.

'I brought us some breakfast,' Spike said, moving to the table beneath the window. Using the paper bag as a plate, he laid out four freshly baked rolls. 'It's gorgeous out there. Feels like spring.'

Zahra stretched out both arms. 'Breakfast in bed with Spike Sanguinetti,' she said sleepily.

'The fishermen are coming in. Looks like they're setting up some kind of market. We could have a walk round; I saw one guy with what looked like a moray eel.'

Zahra sat up, blinking, as though only now aware of where she was. She yawned, showing rows of sharp white teeth. Glancing at her wrist, she realised it was bare. 'What time is it?'

'About a quarter to eight.'

She stared ahead, then shot up, a lithe dark streak as she searched for her clothes.

'What?' Spike laughed. He caught a crinkle of tanned stomach as she bent down to pick up her knickers.

'*Naik*,' Zahra cursed in Arabic.

'Can I help?'

'I'm late.'

'What for?'

'The Citizenship Office opens at eight. The queues will be huge.'

'Are you working?'

'My visa's about to expire,' she said as she pulled her dress over her head.

Spike stared down at the rolls on the table, feeling his appetite ebb. 'What a coincidence.'

Zahra stopped dressing, one hand steadying herself on the bedside table. 'What did you say?'

'Nothing.'

She walked over.

'I thought you were in a hurry.'

'I want you to repeat what you just said.'

'Well . . . we've slept together in three different countries now, Zahra. Every time, the event has been closely followed by a request to help you apply for a visa.'

She glared down. For the first time, she looked her thirty-five years. 'I never asked you to help me get to Europe. You offered, I accepted, but I never asked.'

'There's no need to shout.'

She swore again in Arabic, then gathered her belongings. 'What you just said is very hurtful,' she said, coming back. 'Do you understand that?' As she turned for the door, her foot collided with the empty bottle of *bajtra*, sending it spinning towards the wall. Spike felt words forming in his mind, but ignored them. The door slammed.

A moment later, he went to the window, waiting for her to emerge outside. A minute passed, then he picked up the empty bottle, catching a medicinal whiff as he placed it on the bedside table. The sheets were still indented with her shape. He touched them and felt a trace of warmth.

From the street below came the sound of a door opening. When Spike returned to the window, she was gone.

14

Spike stood hunched in the bath, the tepid shower drizzle barely wetting his hair. As he dressed, he saw that Zahra had left her watch behind. He picked it up, feeling its weight, checking the reverse for an engraving from John the American. *Every blessing*, perhaps. Nothing but a fine dark wrist-hair caught in the strap. After slipping the watch into his pocket, he threw the bread rolls in the bin and left the room.

Downstairs at the desk, he handed over the key and removed his wallet.

'Your friend took care of it,' the receptionist said.

It wasn't a fish market outside but stalls flogging tourist trinkets – miniature Maltese crosses, a stand of enamel key rings with Eyes of Osiris on the fobs. Spike followed the signs to the bus stop, thinking of the work he had to do this morning: an appointment with the Mifsud family accountant, a meeting with the local lawyer. A moment later, he stopped, heart pumping, as though someone had spiked his drink. 'You stupid *charavaca*,' he said aloud to himself in *yanito*.

Her phone rang straight through to voicemail. There was a delay before the beep. 'Zahra,' he said. 'I'm an idiot. A total idiot. Will you call me back? Please . . . I'm sorry.'

He continued to the bus stop, then remembered he'd forgotten to mention her watch.

✳

The man stares down as the girl takes her seat in the back garden of the bar. She looks uneasy, then glances over at a family of three at a corner table – kid blowing Coke bubbles through a straw – and seems to relax.

Still watching from above, the man moves closer to the window.

That black Arabic hair, cut short to look European. The frumpy cardigan to conceal the clinging summer dress. Funny how you can always tell, the man thinks with a grin, however much they try and hide it. Just a glimpse from a distance – the curve of a hip, the angle of a shoulder.

The girl draws up her sleeve and gazes down at her wrist. As if surprised to find it bare, she reaches into her handbag and takes out her phone, staring at the screen so intently that she doesn't seem to register the family leaving the garden, nor the scrape of the bar's back door being bolted behind her.

Chapter Six

The pall-bearers lowered the first coffin into the tomb. There was a clack as the brass runners hit the stone base, then they slid out the ropes and moved to the next coffin, pausing briefly to catch their breath.

Spike peered down. At the edge of the tomb, he could see the shadows of the urns containing the remains of his Maltese grandparents. He'd just paid a substantial amount to have their coffins cremated; the ashes had now been sealed into vessels the size of a jam jar. As in the rest of Malta, space in family tombs was at such a premium that the luxury of a coffin could only be enjoyed until the next generation arrived.

The priest continued his routine in Latin, bowing his head as he spoke, 'dolor' being the only word Spike could make out, in keeping with the name of the cemetery itself, the Addolorata, Our Lady of the Sorrows. The priest's tone was perfunctory, reminding Spike of Assistant Commissioner Azzopardi's comments on the Church's view of suicides.

The Baron was standing with his hands behind his back, a few strands of faded hair fluttering in the breeze blowing in off the rocky hills beyond. The Baroness loomed above him, silk handkerchief dabbing at rouged cheeks, Rufus beside her, as thin and desiccated as the stone crosses that adorned some of the grander tombs behind. A few old friends, the family lawyer and a distant cousin completed the Mifsud mourners.

The priest switched to English. 'Ashes to ashes,' he said, bending down for some soil, 'dust to dust . . .'

Spike scanned the rest of the graveyard. Tapering cypresses cast a dappled light on the pathways. Headless stone angels stood vigil. To the rear of the semicircle, looking away as Spike met his eye, was John Petrovic, all combed blond hair and preppy sports jacket, like a sophomore on his way to a varsity game.

There was a thud as the priest threw a wad of dirt down into the tomb. A nod to the mourners and a small step backwards invited them to do the same. Spike saw the Baroness staring at him; realising he was the closest blood relative, he gathered up a handful of dust, seeping it through his closed fist into Rufus's palm like sand from an hourglass. Rufus tossed it outwards; they all watched in silence as it blew back towards him in the breeze.

A crunch of high heels on gravel broke the spell. Spike turned to see a woman in dark glasses striding up the path. For a few seconds he thought it was Zahra, but as the woman came closer, his sense of relief faded. He managed a half-smile, and Rachel Cassar nodded back.

Once the priest had said a final prayer, the pall-bearers coiled up their ropes and moved away. Spike stared at the lid of the tomb lying on the path. Freshly carved was the short and unsentimental inscription Rufus had chosen:

DAVID MIFSUD, AGED 63,
TERESA MIFSUD, AGED 66.
RIP.

2

Three black Mercedes estates waited in the cemetery car park. Rufus held open a door, ushering the Baron and Baroness into the cool leather-seated interior.

'I'm sorry I was late.'

Spike turned at the sound of a female voice. The chief curator averted her eyes, sensing his disappointment. 'My bus broke down.'

'I thought they were meant to work these days.'

Rachel shrugged. 'I ought to have driven.'

Rufus was gesturing impatiently at the car door. 'Son?'

'We're going to the wake now,' Spike said to Rachel. 'Light refreshments at Rubino's. You'll join us?'

'I don't want to intrude.'

'You wouldn't.' He looked beyond her to the car park. The only other vehicle was a red Chevrolet jeep. Above its rear bumper was a Christian fish sticker, a tiny crucifix signifying the eye.

'There's space for you with us,' Spike said.

'Are you sure?'

'Dad, this is Rachel Cassar. Used to work with Uncle David.'

Once Rufus had managed to focus, a leer took over, a new development with pretty women that Spike found particularly alarming.

'In you come, Rebecca.'

'But what will you –'

'I'll catch you up,' Spike said, turning and setting off towards the jeep.

3

'Stick of gum?'

Spike shook his head. Through the jeep windscreen he made out the pall-bearers working another coffin from a hearse.

'Naked come we into the world, and naked go we also out,' John declared.

Spike thought he recognised the model of coffin from the brochure he and Rufus had perused. 'Or clad in mock pine veneer.'

'Say what?'

The hearse crept away, post-partum, and John turned on the engine. A snatch of heavy metal burst from the sound system; he reached forward and switched it off. 'Sorry,' he muttered as he eased the jeep into automatic.

They pulled onto a roundabout, the engine giving off a throaty, expensive hum. For a charity worker, John seemed to be operating with a hefty disposable income. In the passenger window, Spike saw a sticker advertising a local bar. He deciphered the Gothic lettering backwards: *PASHA*.

'It was a nice service,' John said as he wove through the traffic. 'The Baron spoke well. I've met him before, you know. He visited the charity office once.' John blew a tiny bubble with his gum, which burst like a blister.

'I was surprised not to see Zahra there,' Spike said.

'You and me both.'

'Any idea where she might be?'

'Haven't heard from her in . . . maybe a couple of days.' John chewed vigorously, quarterback's jaw pumping. Bags hung beneath his eyes; Spike saw dots of blood dried into the fresh razorburn on his neck.

'Hasn't she been teaching at the camps?'

He slotted on a pair of black Wayfarers. 'When she came back from Gozo she seemed a bit upset. I thought she could handle some time off.'

Spike felt in his suit pocket for her watch. 'I'm flying home tomorrow.'

'Shame. You'll miss Carnival.'

'I wondered if you might –'

The radio exploded to life with what sounded like a traffic update in Maltese. John listened, then hung a sudden left, following the road that circumvented Valletta beneath its sea walls.

Spike returned the watch to his pocket. 'Have you got Zahra's home address?'

'You have her mobile, don't you?'

They plunged into a tunnel through the base of the city walls. To the right, Spike saw what looked like a row of empty warehouses.

'Yes, but I can't seem to reach her.'

John smiled apologetically. 'I can't just give out an employee's address, buddy. Data protection, you know?'

Spike felt his stomach lurch as they cleared the limestone kink in the middle of Valletta's promontory. A moment later they mounted a narrow pavement, then came to a halt.

Behind, the cortège of Mercedes was drawing up. 'When you've been in Malta as long as me,' John said, checking his blond fringe in the rear-view mirror, 'you learn the short cuts.'

Judging by his response to the traffic report, he'd also picked up more of the local language than he liked to let on. Spike squeezed through the gap between the car door and the wall, then joined the line of mourners waiting to go in for the wake.

4

The grey-haired restaurant owner was assiduous in his attentions to the Baron and Baroness. Framed black-and-white photos on the walls showed other of Malta's illustrious patrons who'd been similarly seduced.

The main dining area was closed for the wake, tables pushed against walls to provide a buffet of wine and a cold collation. Spike caught the eye of the Mifsud family lawyer, then went to gather the beneficiaries – John, the Baron, David's distant cousin.

A cramped rear staircase led to a box-room office. The lawyer sat at the desk as the others positioned themselves opposite. Spike closed the door and joined them.

'Firstly,' the lawyer said, 'I'd like to thank Mr Sanguinetti for his most thorough execution of the wills.' He met Spike's eye and pouted. His dark beard was closely clipped, just a millimetre too long to be classed as stubble. 'In the absence of children or dependants,' he went on, 'Dr Mifsud left his estate to his wife. Teresa Mifsud left hers to the NGO for which she had been a volunteer for the last five years. The sum remaining in their joint account has been used to pay residual liabilities and legal fees. His Lordship, Baron Malaspina, has waived any outstanding rent on the flat, which is exceedingly –'

The Baron swatted away the impending compliment.

'Leaving just the contents of the flat to be auctioned off, proceeds to go to the Mission of St John Hospitaller, of which Mr John Petrovic here is trustee. Otherwise . . .' The lawyer glanced up. 'Mr Sanguinetti?'

Spike turned to the cousin. 'If there are any small things you'd like. Mementoes.'

'How do I get them?' the cousin said cheerfully. His collar was too tight around his neck. Blue tattoos bruised the knuckles of his right hand.

'There's an estate agent coming to the flat tomorrow morning to look into renting it out,' the Maltese lawyer said, nose crinkling in distaste. 'I suppose you could come by then.'

The cousin bowed at the lawyer, as though used to attending court, then left.

'Now I just need the keys to the flat,' the lawyer said to Spike.
'Maybe I should be there,' Spike said. 'Let in the estate agent myself.'
'As you wish.' The lawyer zipped up his calfskin pouch, then caressed his beard. 'Now,' he said, looking back at Spike. 'A drink?'

5

The wake began to liven up once a few carafes of Maltese white had done the rounds. Rufus was chatting to Rachel Cassar as a coterie of local worthies paid homage to the Baron. The Maltese lawyer kept trying to catch Spike's eye, so he pulled out his mobile and stepped onto the street.

Again, Zahra's phone rang directly to voicemail. He left a terse message about her watch, also mentioning his departure time the next day.

A tour group had gathered outside the Baron's palazzo, admiring a statue in a niche on its corner, an apostle with his index and middle fingers raised, forming the sign of the cross. Spike walked past them and unlocked the door to the Mifsud flat.

His reflection beamed back from the hallway mirror. Sprigs of grey coiled at his temples; in no time at all, he thought as he moved into the sitting room, he'd be Uncle David's age.

The address book was still in the drawer; he opened it up and tore out Zahra's entry. From the edge of the desk, David and Teresa laughed back from their honeymoon photo, prompting Spike to remember how, as a child, he'd always been perplexed by the smiling images of murder victims on the news. He picked up the photo frame and tucked it under one arm.

A noise came from behind. 'Hello?' he called out.

The noise came again, more subtle now. The wooden floor above, Spike assumed – Clara the maid, cleaning the palazzo while the Baron and Baroness were out. As he passed the bedroom, he looked inside. Teresa's ball gown lay on the floor. Hadn't that been on the bed before?

Unsettled now, Spike hurried to the front door, relieved to find the city still going about its humdrum business outside.

6

The Baroness watched approvingly as Spike positioned the photo frame on the buffet table. 'Bravo,' she called out, raising her glass. The other mourners fell silent. 'To happier times,' she said, and everyone repeated the toast.

'That was thoughtful,' came a voice.

Spike turned to see Rachel Cassar at his shoulder. Her herring-bone-check skirt emphasised her narrow waist and rounded hips. She seemed to have left her spectacles at home.

'You escaped my father.'

'He was the perfect gentleman.'

Rachel declined some wine, so Spike topped up his own glass, downing it then filling it again.

'Only way to get through these things,' Rachel said uncertainly. She turned to look at the room. 'I didn't realise David was so close to the mighty Malaspinas.'

'Teresa and he rented their apartment from them. It's part of their palazzo.'

'Not sure my landlord will come to my funeral,' Rachel said, glancing at the Baron, who was standing in front of the photo-graph, resolutely ignoring an elderly man trying to catch his ear.

'Did David do much work in Gozo?'

Rachel turned. 'I doubt it. They have their own cathedral museum. Why?'

'He photographed a painting there before his death. From the chapel of St Agatha. The painting seems to have vanished.'

'How do you mean "vanished"?'

'It was missing from the chapel wall.'

Rachel paused. 'Isn't that where a priest died?'

Spike nodded, then finished his wine.

'Photographs, you say?'

'Photographs.'

'Can you show them to me?'

'They're in my hotel room.' She held his eye. 'Our hotel room,' he added, glancing over at his father, who was roosting alone now on his chair.

'Well, if you do want me to take a look, I'll be at home all evening.'

The Baroness was coming towards them through the crowd. Spike felt something slipped into his jacket pocket. When he looked round, Rachel was heading for the door.

'My darlink,' the Baroness said. Her cream blouse revealed a papery sternum watermarked with veins. Her eyes sparkled with a sad beauty.

'Do you have a spare key for David's flat?' Spike asked.

The Baroness gave a frown. 'No. There is only one set. Why?'

'No reason.'

'That was why the police needed to break in,' she said, stepping closer. 'Nineteenth-century ironmongery, too expensive to copy. Why, you have lost them?'

Spike shook his head. 'Thanks for coming. Both of you.'

7

Spike led Rufus along the cobbles, his father's scrawny arm tucked beneath his own.

'Well, I thought that went well,' Rufus said.

'It did, Dad.'

Steering him into the lobby, Spike received an approving smile from the pretty female receptionist.

'You know,' Rufus said as he entered the lift, 'not one person at the wake believed David capable of such a crime. I told them my boy was looking into it. That he'd get to the bottom of things. My kind, clever boy.'

In the room, Rufus sat on his bed as Spike prepared his tablets. 'Oh yes,' he sighed as he rolled beneath the covers. 'Fresh sheets. Wonderful. Just wonderful.'

After tucking him in, Spike went to his own bed. The first snore arrived within moments, a sound he used to loathe, but which now he found oddly comforting.

Switching on his phone, he expected a flurry of apologetic messages from Zahra. Just the same screensaver of the Rock. He dialled her number: voicemail.

After lying down for a minute, he picked up his jacket and took out the business card that Rachel Cassar had slipped into his pocket.

✳

She is unsure if she is awake or asleep. A word keeps seeping through her mind – '*mawlud . . . mawlud*' – sometimes in her dreams, sometimes loud and real, as though someone close by is whimpering. She feels hands grabbing her, plunging beneath her armpits, dragging her across the stone floor.

Cold water splashes down, wetting her hair, chilling her neck and shoulders. She lets her bladder go and feels the brief warmth of relief. Her bowels slacken and more water is sloshed on, combined with a deeper voice, laughter and catcalls.

Her armpits sting as she is hauled from the cold and placed on a mattress. Her head sinks into prickly blankets. Time passes.

She gives a moan. Spike is with her; she can feel his strong fingers working between her thighs. She sighs, pressing her face down into the bed, ignoring the scratch of the blankets on her cheeks as she pushes back against him. His hands are on her spine now, grabbing her breasts. Too rough . . . she tries to turn but he is holding her down. The hacking clearance of a throat, a spatter of saliva between her buttocks . . . A pain sears her insides; he is hurting her, so she cries out, then starts to reach behind, feeling not Spike's muscled leg but a flaccid thigh, moist and hairy, as the laughter comes again, and now she struggles properly, but more hands are on her, shoving her onto the bed as the heat burns back and forth, until she screams, and a hand covers her mouth, a needle biting into her thigh, face slumping, tears spilling from her eyes, the stinking blankets too coarse to absorb them.

Arms shift her again.

'*Mawlud*,' she hears. '*Mawlud*.'

Something is slipped into her mouth. Her saliva softens it and she tastes the sweet paste of a biscuit. A bottle is raised to her mouth, water sluiced inside. She gulps hard, then slumps back onto her side, that word creeping into her dreams again, embroidering her nightmares.

She half opens her eyes. She is naked, sitting against a gate, legs out, a stinging pain in her rectum which pulsates in time with her heartbeat. The back of her head is propped between two metal bars; as she turns, she sees another woman beside her, dressed in a hospital gown, head lolling, long black hair lank and greasy. The woman grasps at her chest, where two dark rings of fluid stain the material of her gown. '*Mawlud*,' she mewls to herself in Arabic. *My baby.*

Chapter Seven

I

Spike found the address two streets down from the Museum of Fine Arts. A rusty silver Skoda was parked outside. He held down the intercom, poised to walk away as a croaky voice answered: 'Hello?' She sounded half asleep.

'Rachel?'

'Yes?'

'It's Spike.'

There was a pause. 'I'm on the second floor.'

The latch snapped and Spike began his ascent up a narrow flight of stairs. Dirty panes revealed another inner courtyard. Sofa cushions rotted on the ground below, spewing foam – Valletta crumbling behind its grand facade. He knocked on her door.

'Just a minute.'

Glancing up the stairwell, he saw a small cat's head with pointy tortoiseshell ears peering down. Footsteps echoed; the door part opened to reveal Rachel Cassar. She wore tartan pyjamas and a ribbed fisherman's jumper.

Spike held out the sleeve of photographs like a bouquet.

'Of course,' she smiled. 'Come in.'

The sitting room had a kitchenette along the left-hand side and the inevitable Maltese balcony at the end.

'Coffee?' Rachel said.

'Anything stronger?'

She frowned through her black-rimmed specs. 'Some *bajtra*?'

'Coffee, then.'

'Or vodka? I think there's some vodka in the freezer. A vodka and Kinnie?'

'Great. Thanks.'

Spike turned and scanned the floor-to-ceiling bookcases. Zahra would have liked this flat, he thought bitterly. On one wall hung a set of modernist prints: cutlery, plates, fruit bowl, brutal in their simplicity. 'Sometimes I get a bit tired of the baroque,' Rachel said as she passed Spike a tumbler. The TV was paused mid-romcom; she found the remote and switched it off. The balcony's net curtains swirled as she curled herself into a well-worn leather armchair.

'Thanks for coming today,' Spike said, choosing the sofa.

'A pleasure. Always an honour to see the Baron.'

'I get the impression you don't like him much.'

'I wouldn't go that far . . .' She reached over and plucked an ashtray from the sofa arm; Spike hadn't realised she smoked. 'I'm just a bit dubious about the Knights of Malta.'

'Why?'

'Grand Masters, secret handshakes: they're no better than Freemasons. Especially when it comes to nepotism.'

'Michael was always very kind to my uncle and aunt.'

'Maybe I'm just an embittered commoner. But I still don't have much time for Baron Malaspina.' She tapped out a B&H and lit it. 'Three years ago,' she said, 'we were looking for sponsorship for a Mattia Preti exhibition at the museum. The Baron's famously well connected, so I put in a call. He said he'd help on one condition. That an external curator was brought in. When I asked why, he told me the native Maltese worked best when guided by outsiders. Apparently history demonstrates that we've always needed strong foreign leadership to thrive. He even gave a list: Phoenicians, Carthaginians, Romans, Arabs, Normans, Knights, Brits. I told him we were more comfortable using local talent, and we never heard from him again.' She inhaled, then smiled; Spike thought she should do it more. 'I enjoyed talking to your father. He knows a lot about art.'

'He knows a lot about a lot of things. Former English teacher. Bluffing is a job requirement.'

'Is he . . .'

'It's called Marfan syndrome. A disorder of the connective tissue. Your joints and muscles are too loose. There's a danger you'll literally fall apart.'

'Has he always had it?'

'It was only diagnosed recently. Sometimes the symptoms don't manifest themselves till late in life.'

Spike sensed Rachel eyeing his long, lean limbs. 'Is it hereditary?'

'It can be.' He drank some vodka and Kinnie; the bitter-sweet local soft drink was one he'd be avoiding in future.

'Sorry,' Rachel laughed. 'I don't think I've made one of those before. I'm not much of a drinker.'

'No wonder you got on with my dad.'

There was a pause. 'Can I see the photographs?' She came and sat beside him on the sofa, giving off a scent of freshly spritzed perfume: sugary as candyfloss, surprising somehow. He opened the sleeve and passed her the first one.

'A pretty average St Agatha,' she said, frowning downwards. 'Some evidence of overpainting. Needs a damn good clean.' She looked up. 'It's definitely Gozitan?'

'From a clifftop chapel. Why would it have interested my uncle?'

'Maybe he was overseeing the cleaning process – even the lowliest church needs to maintain its artwork.'

'But why photograph this one?'

Rachel looked down again. 'Malta's full of paintings like this. Do you know the story?'

'I know she's your patron saint,' Spike said, aware he was quoting a taxi driver.

'One of our patron saints,' Rachel corrected. 'There's also St Paul and St Publius. Then there's the fact that during World War II, the German and Italian siege was broken on the day of the Assumption. So we like to think Mary looks out for us too.'

'Another miracle.'

'Another?'

'The bomb that never went off.'

Rachel gave a snort. 'You probably don't know the whole story. Later, when they opened up the bomb, they found a note inside: "Greetings from Plzeň." It had been made in the Skoda factory, and the Czech workers had been filling the munitions with sand instead of explosives.'

'Is that why you drive a Skoda?'

'As a reminder that human intervention is more reliable than divine?' Rachel's face opened into another smile, then she straightened her spectacles on her nose. 'Back to St Agatha. She was a noblewoman from third-century Sicily. A famous beauty. The Roman governor took a shine to her. She fled across the water to Malta, but he dragged her back and locked her in a brothel. He tried to seduce her but failed. So he maimed her. Guess which type of cancer she's the patron saint of?'

'Are you serious?'

'Not how I'd want a double mastectomy, but there you have it.'

Spike took another hit of perfume as Rachel pulled off her jumper. Underneath she wore a ribbed white T-shirt. No bra, he noted like a schoolboy before turning back to the photos. 'These ones are a bit blurred . . .'

Rachel edged closer, then took the whole pile. 'They look like infrared images. Were there more?'

'Yes, but I lost them.'

'*Lost* them?'

'Someone tried to shove me into the St James Ditch. A few fell down.'

She gave a puzzled glance, then continued sifting. 'They're expensive. You need to rent equipment, pay development costs . . .'

'This I know,' Spike muttered.

'Why didn't you go down and pick them up?'

'You try climbing down there. Anyway, they're gone now.'

She didn't seem to be listening. 'Why would David Mifsud have wasted IR images on some workaday painting from Gozo?' she murmured out loud.

'You tell me . . . Rachel?'

She looked back up. 'IR is normally used by an expert looking for something beneath the paint. The camera flash gives off infrared radiation – if there are traces of carbon beneath the paint, a particular type of film will pick it up. You get to see pencil lines, preliminary sketches. Or a palimpsest – one image on top of another.'

'A bit like Malta.'

'Sorry?'

'Arabs, Normans, Knights . . .'

She stared at him blankly, as though baffled to find him capable of analogy.

'I don't see any pencil lines there,' Spike said, looking back at the photos, which Rachel continued to shuffle through like a conjuror.

'The flash isn't powerful enough to capture an entire painting. You need to get in close to the paintwork; focus on one part at a time. Then you can slot the images together like a jigsaw.'

'Can we try that now?'

'Not if you've lost some of the photos. There's a computer program back at the museum. I could scan the photos in, fit them together. I'm there from lunchtime tomorrow. Any good?'

'Afraid not. We're flying home to Gib.'

'Jib?'

'Gibraltar.'

'Can I hang on to them? Give you a call?'

'You're a saint.'

'Please; anything but that.' She fixed him pointedly through her glasses. 'Fancy a top-up?'

He turned, looking out at the bookshelves, thinking again of Zahra. She hadn't even turned up for the funerals. One petty argument and she'd chosen to overlook all the kindness David and Teresa had shown her. Unbelievable . . . 'Why not?' he said, holding out his glass.

'So what was that about the St James Ditch?' Rachel asked as she mixed his drink.

'I seem to have upset someone local.'

'That happens a lot, does it?' she said as she returned to the sofa, 'in *Gib*?'

'You'd be surprised. The Spanish hate us. British squaddies are always spoiling for a fight. It's a violent place to grow up.'

'So you're just a street thug?'

'Of the vilest sort.'

Rachel's lips parted, glittering with a gloss which seemed to have been mysteriously applied. 'Then I'll have to keep my eye on you,' she said, shifting closer on the sofa. 'Cheers, Spike Sanguinetti.'

'Cheers.'

2

Hair unkempt, still wearing his suit, Spike paced through Valletta, sensing glances from the early-morning office workers who were now streaming into the city. Waiting outside the flat was a furniture remover, a stack of flattened boxes propped against the facade. 'Late night, was it?' he said, glancing at his watch. 'The estate agent's already left.'

Spike let him into the flat. 'Anything I've marked with a red sticker goes for auction. The unmarked stuff you can chuck away.' Spike licked his lips, then put a hand to his mouth, seeing a smear of glittery gloss come away on his fingers. 'The Madonna and Child up there is thought to be a Baglione. Be careful with it.'

He turned for the door, but the remover called after him. Though a short man, he had the tough, wiry frame of a jockey. He dipped into his overalls and held out an envelope. 'The estate agent wanted you to have this.'

Inside were two latchkeys, both labelled with an address in Valletta. 'What is it?'

'They're for a property. By the Italian Auberge.'

'What kind of property?'

'Fucked if I know, mate,' the remover said as he turned to a depiction of the Ascension and wrenched it roughly from the wall.

3

The Italian Auberge now housed the Ministry of Tourism. Head throbbing, Spike found the address down an alley to its side. The bell pushes suggested the building was being used by local professionals supplementing their income through private tutoring. 'Dr David Vasallo, BSc, MA,' said one, 'One-on-One Classes, All Sciences to A Level'.

Spike unlocked the door to number 16. The room was unfurnished save for a Van Gogh-style wicker chair and a cheap wooden easel. Though the easel was facing away, Spike could already see that the stretcher upon it was oval-shaped.

He edged towards it past a crate of tubes, brushes and solvents. The painting was unfinished – half the canvas still blank – but

Spike recognised its subject matter. So Mifsud had been making a copy of the Gozo 'St Agatha'. Not a very good copy – colours too bright, faces clumsily rendered – but at least Spike now had an explanation for the photographs. The impetuous young man who had laid down his brush in a fit of pique had decided to resume painting after his retirement. Why he'd started with this unexceptional version of St Agatha was unclear, but there it was – Uncle David returning to his first love.

Spike put the easel, stretcher and crate inside a cardboard box. Maybe they would do as a memento for the distant cousin. The chair could wait for the next tenant, he thought to himself as he locked up.

4

Spike dropped off the box and keys at the flat, then headed through the City Gate towards Floriana. It took a few minutes to locate Zahra's address, a humble set of rooms above a grocer's. She wasn't answering her buzzer, so he went into the shop below and negotiated an extortionate rate for the purchase of a single envelope and biro.

He sealed her watch inside, then scribbled a message on the back, mentioning only the time of his flight and his mobile number in case she had misplaced it.

Back at the hotel, Rufus was still in bed. 'Been with your old friend again?' he said archly as he slid a skin-clad bone from between the sheets.

'Something like that.'

They caught a taxi to the airport. An hour later, Spike stepped out of the boarding queue and phoned Rachel. Perhaps she was still sleeping off last night: straight to voicemail. With a craven sense of relief, he left her a message, filling her in on Mifsud's rented art studio, and the fact that he'd been copying the Gozo painting. Back in the queue, he felt his phone vibrate. A Maltese number; he ducked aside to answer. 'Rachel?'

'Spike?'

'Yes.'

'This is Chen.'

'Who?'

'I have envelope. With the watch.'

Spike moved away to the glass partition which divided the gate from Arrivals. Above the exit, a banner welcomed tourists to 'Malta Carnival – Introduced by Knights, Enjoyed by Nights'. Fire the copywriter, Spike thought. 'You live with Zahra, right?' he said.

'Flat-mate,' she replied, splitting the word with Oriental precision.

'Is she with you now?'

'Gone.'

'Gone where?'

'Not sure. I think she leave with boyfriend.'

'Which boyfriend?'

'You?'

Spike glanced back at the queue, where his father was nearing the front. 'When did you last see her?'

'Friday.'

'*Friday*? So Zahra hasn't been home for five days?'

'Her passport is gone. I thought maybe you had both left for trip.'

'Have you had any contact from her since?'

'No.'

Spike heard his father's voice echoing through the terminal: he was trying to keep his place in the queue without surrendering his boarding pass. 'Chen,' Spike said, 'you have to report this to the police. To Assistant Commissioner Azzopardi. Do you understand?'

'Yes.'

'Tell them Zahra is missing. That you haven't seen her since Friday.' He heard his name called; Rufus's cheeks reddened as irate travellers jostled him from behind.

'Can you do that for me, Chen?'

'I try.'

Spike hung up and returned to the queue.

'You see?' Rufus said. 'My boy's here.' He held out his boarding pass.

'Something's come up, Dad.'

'We can talk on the flight.'

'No, we can't.'

'Why not?'

'Because I'm not getting on the plane.'

✠

She tries to move but something is holding her back. She looks down and in the half-light sees ropes around her elbows, looped through the metal bars, keeping her in a seated position, numbing her arms through lack of blood.

A sound comes from in front, and she lowers her head, squinting at a glimmer of light: the gates are opening, figures moving against a bright backdrop. Her eyes sting, then the gates close again and she hears voices, a creak of springs as a deadweight is lowered onto a camp bed.

Footsteps now; she closes her eyes, feeling a hand grab at her hair, hoisting up her chin. A fingertip presses down on her eyeball, easing up the lid. She sees a silhouette above, a jaw cut out against the gloom. Her head lolls and the man releases her, barking something in Maltese. She keeps her eyes closed, trying to control her breathing, trying not to scream. Screaming makes it worse.

Footsteps again, then a bolt scraping roughly back in place.

She reopens her eyes, peering down at her arms, at the

thickness of the rope. The knot is large and complex, some kind of fisherman's loop. She stretches her fingers towards it but they will not reach. She tries her other hand. The dizziness returns; she shivers despite the warm sweat trickling down her face.

When she next awakens, groans are spreading through the cavern as the needles are administered. She wishes she were alone in the dark. There is no comfort in the cries of others.

Chapter Eight

I

Giving up on the taxi queue, Spike caught a bendy bus back to Valletta. Azzopardi's mobile phone was engaged, so he left him a message telling him to expect a visit from Chen. In the row in front, a batch of rookie tourists, fresh off the plane, stared out at the newsagents' signs offering 'London Newspapers Today', wondering aloud to each other about Malta's current colonial status.

Drumming his foot as the bus waited at a set of temporary lights, Spike called Jessica in Gibraltar. Her tone suggested there was a limit to her benevolence, but she agreed to meet Rufus off the plane and drive him home to Chicardo's. 'What do you mean *gone*?' she said when Spike told her about Zahra's disappearance.

'She's not answering her phone. Her flatmate hasn't seen her in five days.'

'And this was after you two hooked up again?'

'Yes.'

'Maybe she's just not interested.'

'I'd prefer that to the alternative.'

Jessica paused. 'Sorry, Spike.'

As soon as the doors opened at the bus terminus, Spike grabbed his bag and pushed through the crowds towards the City Gate.

2

Not even a double room was available at the hotel, so Spike went to the estate agent's office and requested the keys back for the flat. On arrival, he found the hallway crammed with packing crates awaiting collection; he edged past into the sitting room and retrieved Mifsud's address book from the desk drawer. John Petrovic's mobile gave a 'no such number' whine. No answer from the charity office landline either. He tried Azzopardi. Finally, a ringtone.

'Mr Sanguinetti.'

'Did you get my message?'

'Yes.'

'And you've spoken to Chen?'

'She's just left the Depot.'

'Has Zahra turned up?'

'The Moroccan?'

'The court interpreter.'

'You do realise she's on a work visa, Mr Sanguinetti.'

'Of course.'

'Which runs out next week.'

'She was going to renew.'

'Well, she didn't. And her passport's still missing. Know what that means?'

'What?'

'That she's someone else's problem. Probably found her way to Sicily like the rest of them.'

'Now you listen to me,' Spike said. 'Zahra's passport's only missing because she took it with her to the visa office on Friday. She's not been seen since and I'm very concerned for her safety.'

'Be grateful she's a migrant, Mr Sanguinetti, or we might have picked you up.'

'Sorry?'

'Her flatmate says you were the last person seen with her. People seem to fall off the grid when you're in town. You're something of a liability.'

'Zahra would not just *disappear*.'

'Plenty of them do, Mr Sanguinetti, every week. Goodbye.'

'*Manascada!*' Spike put his fingers to his temples and tried to think. There was one place left to try. He pocketed the address book, then left the flat.

3

A night flight rumbled overhead as Spike skirted the perimeter fence. Two hangar-sized buildings loomed on the other side. The site of a former British Army barracks, John had said. Spike found the main entrance and stopped.

The gateposts were bound together by a bicycle lock. The barbed wire at the top looked like a hangover from the military era. He touched the gate tentatively in case it held a charge, then gave it a firmer shake. It parted, but not widely enough to squeeze through. Evidently the inhabitants of the family camp did not enjoy the right to enter and exit at will.

Continuing along the fence, he searched for gaps, then turned around and set off up the verge he and Zahra had followed on their last visit.

A scent of woodsmoke wafted from ahead, an orange glow. Voices on the breeze, the tinny chime of music. Spike hesitated, then carried on walking.

The bonfire was burning in the wasteland behind the Portakabin. Thirty or so figures flickered in its flames, female voices combining with male.

Adjusting his gait to casual, Spike strolled towards the circle. The music was coming from a mobile phone on full volume. Plastic bottles were being passed around, along with what smelled like a cannabis bong.

As Spike came closer, an athletic man snapped his hands to the ground and sprang up. Nearby conversations stopped; hostile faces turned.

The man took a step towards Spike. He wore a red baseball cap low over his eyes, presumably to protect them from the smoke.

Spike held out his palms. 'I'm looking for Zahra.'

A seated man barked something in Arabic, raising a modest laugh. The man in the baseball cap stepped closer.

'She's a teacher here,' Spike said, taking out a photograph. 'Has anyone seen her?' One of the revellers picked some leaves off a sprig, then folded them into his mouth like a stick of gum.

'Anyone?' Spike repeated as he moved along the line of people. Roasting at the edge of the fire was a spit. Drawing closer, Spike made out the long, charred shape of a rabbit. He crouched down to the woman turning it. 'Do you remember me?' he said. 'I was here with Zahra last week.'

The woman turned her face away so Spike could only see the back of her headscarf.

'You mistook her for Dinah. Do you remember?'

A louder voice came from the other side of the fire. Spike heard 'Dinah' repeated in various tones until a thicker-set man climbed to his feet. 'What you say for Dinah?' he shouted, accent West African rather than Arabic. His nostrils flared.

'I'm looking for Zahra,' Spike said, and the heavier man shoved him in the chest, sending him staggering back towards the bonfire, regaining his balance moments before tipping into the flames. He straightened up slowly.

When the African came at him again, Spike moved to one side. The man's momentum carried him on, so Spike stuck out a foot.

The man stumbled, then fell to the ground. More laughter from the revellers.

'I don't want to fight,' Spike said. 'I just want information.'

Someone killed the music. Four youths rose from the fire. One held a carving knife, its blade gleaming with rabbit fat.

'Go,' the big man called up. 'Now.'

Spike backed away towards the Portakabin.

4

The door to the Portakabin was locked, no signs of life inside. Spike glanced back at the bonfire, seeing only sparks and smoke flowing upwards into the sky.

He stopped. A noise had come from the side of the steps. '*Pst*,' he heard. '*Ici*.'

Spike moved to the edge of the platform. A clearing had been formed between the Portakabin and the perimeter fence, weeds and creepers tamped down, a blanket spread over the ground. In one corner a man sat crouching on his hunkers. Jaundiced eyes flashed in the moonlight.

'*Ici, mec*,' the man whispered.

'Frankie?'

'*Oui, c'est Frankie*.' A shy smile: '*Comme Frank Sinatra, mais plus beau*.'

Spike stepped down into the clearing.

'*Plus vite*,' Frankie whispered.

A tang of stale urine mixed with the humid earth as Spike moved towards him. Frankie motioned for Spike to duck down further until they faced each other like a couple of squatting Buddhas.

'*C'est bien*.'

The sores around Frankie's mouth had multiplied. 'No French,' Spike said. 'Remember?'

'Engleesh,' Frankie replied as he stretched an arm into the undergrowth by the fence. His hand returned with a plastic tub. '*Cherchez la femme*,' he said as he prised his fingers beneath the lid. '*C'est toujours la femme qu'il faut chercher.*'

Spike started to stand.

'You like khat?' Frankie asked slowly as the lid to the tub came off. Cigarette butts, most of them hand-rolled, an inch or so of tobacco remaining.

'I don't smoke,' Spike said, turning away.

'*Zahra*,' came a whisper.

Spike stopped. 'What did you say?'

Frankie itched at his mouth with an uncut thumbnail as Spike crouched down beside him. 'You've seen Zahra?' he said.

Frankie grinned.

'When?'

'Friday.'

'Where?'

'*Ici.* Here.'

'Working? Teaching?'

'In the night-time.' He pointed up at the Portakabin. 'Frankie hearing things.'

Spike moved closer. 'What did you hear?'

'*L'Américain.*'

'John?'

'*Oui, Jean.* Shouting. Angry.'

Spike glanced to the left. The clearing was out of sight of the Portakabin but well within earshot. 'What were they shouting about?'

Frankie sniggered, covering his mouth with a hand. '*Jean*,' he said. 'He liking *les jeunes*. Young girls.' He made a half-thrust with his hips. 'Frankie too . . . and now look!' He lifted up his woollen jumper: looped around his belly was a flaky band of fuchsia sores. '*Le pauvre Frankie,*' he groaned, '*avec les sales jeunes . . .*'

A crunch of gravel came from behind; multiple footsteps. Frankie dropped his jumper down. '*Viens,*' he hissed, '*vite.*' Voices now; the glow of a torch.

Frankie crawled into the right-hand corner of the clearing. A passageway of flattened undergrowth extended as Spike followed behind, keeping his head close to the fusty ground.

When they reached the perimeter fence, Frankie shuffled to the side, hoisting up the base of the wire for Spike to squeeze beneath. The voices grew louder; Spike felt the mesh scrape against his back. Once on the other side, he crawled forward, then stood.

Frankie's sore-spattered face clattered against the wire. 'Baby girl,' he hissed. 'Twelve, maybe fourteen year. You know?'

5

The taxi stopped at the end of a pedestrianised street in St Julian's. 'Up there on the left,' the cabbie said. 'You can't miss it.'

Spike made use of a cashpoint, then set off down the corridor of flashing neon. A few of the bars seemed to be closed for the off season, but most had music throbbing from within, the odd early-bird drinker already slumped at the counter.

Pasha occupied the last berth on the strip. A guest-list queuing area was roped off, an act of some optimism in a deserted street. Spike ducked beneath and found the door closed. When he lowered the handle, it opened easily.

The cloakroom was empty, a single spotlight illuminating the attendant's stool. Two hanging Bedouin rugs blocked the route past; Spike slipped between them to find a darkened dance floor, chairs stacked to one side, DJ booth with the door ajar. The bar was encrusted with chipped mosaic tiles depicting a sultan's palace. Maltese pop played from a battery-operated radio on the shelf behind.

A painfully thin girl in a Ramones T-shirt appeared from the curtain at the side of the bar, carrying a plastic-wrapped tray of supermarket Coke. Her hair was henna red, tied back to reveal a shaven underside.

Nodding to the music, she gave a jump as she saw Spike standing with his arms folded on the other side of the bar. 'Jesus,' she blurted in an American accent, putting down the tray of cans. 'We're not open till ten.'

Spike stared at her across the bar. There was so much metal in her face it looked as though she'd been caught in a nail bomb and the doctors had decided not to operate.

'You fucking *slow*?' she said to Spike, who still hadn't moved. She withdrew a biro from her ponytail and stabbed it through the plastic of the tray.

'I'm looking for John Petrovic.'

'Well, he ain't here, sweetheart,' the barmaid said, ripping back the casing.

'But he'll be in later, right?'

'When we're open you can pay the fifteen-euro cover charge and find out for yourself.'

She took out a can, then glanced up. 'You need to leave. *Now*. The bouncer's out back.'

Spike reached slowly into his pocket. 'Thing is,' he said, 'I owe John money, but I'm on a flight home tonight.' He slid three folded notes across the bar.

'Mango Lounge,' the barmaid said, jabbing the biro back into her ponytail. 'On the seafront.'

6

The strip on the beachfront was busier. Girls with promotional leaflets darted from bars like fish at a lure. A brunette in hot pants and a tied-off man's shirt stepped in front of Spike. 'Free chaser with every pint,' she said in a London accent.

'I'm too broke.'

'Babe, I'd buy you a drink any time,' she replied, tapping him on the behind with her sheaf of flyers.

The bars occupied the ground floors of what looked like holiday apartments. The odd party was taking place on the balconies above, but mostly the windows were dark. Spike passed a group of students talking German, all carrying balloons on sticks. Below on the beach, a couple disappeared hand in hand along a carpet of moonlight.

Louder music throbbed ahead, 'Mango Lounge' scribbled in orange neon above a doorway. Inside, a waitress stood on the bar, firing a water pistol of tequila down into the mouths of three underage European boys, their pimply heads tilted back like nestlings. Watching on unimpressed was a group of tall, vanilla-haired Scandinavian girls.

Spike moved deeper inside the room. Vicious nu-metal pumped from speakers. In one corner sat a pack of groomed Maltese youths, eking out bottles of Cisk beer, their fitted shirts and complex facial hair suggesting an affiliation with the Italian national football team. A few ruddy-faced British ex-pats were huddled round a quiz machine, too old for the scene but seeming not to care.

Spike checked the booths on the far wall. In one sat a blond man with a freckled American face.

One of the Scandinavians nudged her friend as Spike passed, but he ignored her, slipping onto the banquette beside John, who had his bulky white trainers up on the table, frowning at a mobile phone as he composed what looked like a lengthy text message.

Spike tapped John hard on the shoulder. The protest died on his lips as he recognised Spike. He managed an unwilling smile. 'Hey, bud,' he shouted above the music. 'I thought you were going home.'

'I'm looking for Zahra.'

He screwed up his face. 'You're what?'

'You heard.'

John removed his feet from the table, then slipped his phone into the pocket of his loose, low-hanging jeans. 'You guys had a thing once. Right?'

In the next-door booth, two of the Germans had broken away from the main group and were kissing greedily, balloon sticks discarded on the floor.

'I get it,' John said, clapping a hand onto Spike's shoulder. 'I'd be the same.'

'Where is she, John?'

They both looked up as the waitress appeared. She mouthed something in Maltese, and John nodded back. 'We need to get you a drink,' he said, rising to his feet. 'I'll grab us both one.'

Spike stood and watched him walk to the bar. The waitress decapitated a first bottle of beer as John reached for his wallet.

'*Abend!*' Spike heard above the music. He glanced round and saw that the rest of the German group had appeared. The kissing couple shrank down in their seats. '*Erwischt!*' someone yelled gleefully.

When Spike looked back, the waitress was tonging wedges of lime into bottle necks. John Petrovic had gone.

Spike plunged forward into the crowd, knocking into a German with a rat's tail, who muttered an incomprehensible insult. 'Your drinks!' the waitress called, but Spike pushed past her into the corridor. Ladies to the left, Gents to the right, security door marked Fire Exit . . . Spike tried the Gents first, seeing one of the tequila boys praying on his hands and knees to the urinal as his friends roared with laughter. The cubicle doors were all open.

The waitress was standing in the corridor. '*Oi!*' she shouted as Spike put his shoulder to the back door and burst outside. On the far pavement stood a figure. 'John!' Spike called out.

The figure turned, then vaulted the barrier to the beach.

7

Spike set off across the road. A souped-up muscle car was coming the other way; it braked in front of him, a hairy bejewelled fist holding down the horn as Spike scrambled over the flame-licked bonnet and hurdled the railings to the beach.

To the left rose sand dunes, to the right a promontory with a few parked cars. The figure was running between them along the edge of the water.

Spike sprinted down the beach, glimpsing a half-naked couple clamped together in a depression in the sand. They froze as he passed, faces fused.

The figure was thirty yards ahead; as Spike reached the furthest extent of the waves, the harder-packed sand allowed him to increase his speed. He was gaining; he heard the regular splash of his feet as they pounded the thin film of tepid water below. 'Petrovic!' he called out.

John glanced round, then stumbled, and Spike picked up his knees higher. A low sea wall flanked the promontory – the car park was part of a spit used to hold the beach in place. John moved diagonally into the softer sand, heading towards a set of steps, but Spike kept along the fringes of the water, cutting in at the last moment and propelling himself into the air. His outstretched hand clipped one of John's oversized trainers, sending him crashing chin first into the sand.

Spike landed painfully on his hands, then sprung to his feet.

John was sitting up now, rubbing wet sand from his hair and eyes. Spike took a step towards him.

'What is your *problem*?' John yelled, clambering up awkwardly. 'Are you *retarded*?' Tendons appeared in his neck and his jaw jutted, as though he were readying himself for the last charge of a football game.

'I asked you a question, Petrovic. Where's Zahra?'

John thrust out his arms in frustration and moved forward, then seemed to take Spike's measure and stop. 'For Christ's sake . . .' He lowered his gaze. 'She was asking me about some girl. OK?'

'Dinah?' Spike said.

'Yeah. Dinah. That's it.' His eyes switched left: at the far end of the beach, the courting couple were hurrying back hand in hand towards the road.

'And where is she now?' Spike said.

'I have no fuckin' idea.' John shook another clod of sand from his baggy denims. 'Are we done?' Flexing his neck, he turned and started walking towards the promontory.

'I know about the girls,' Spike called after.

John hesitated, then continued walking.

'The underage girls.'

John slowed. Spike watched his shoulders move up and down as he tried to catch his breath.

'I'm sure the US embassy will be fascinated to hear about a charity worker with a penchant for child abuse.'

John turned to the left, towards the sea. A moment passed. 'It isn't what you think,' he said as Spike moved towards him, fists tucked beneath biceps.

'The girl came onto *me*, right?' John resumed. 'I'd only just got to Malta. No more Peace Corps; I was lonely. She told me she was legal, but then the texts started coming. Photos of us together.' John paused, the only sound now the steady rhythmic whisper of the Mediterranean. 'I changed cell but they kept on coming. I've got a girl back in the States, you know?' His voice took on a whining, childlike quality. 'Then another text arrived. He told me he could make it stop.'

'Who could?'

'The man sending the pictures.'

'What was his name?'

'We never met.'

'His name?'

John turned his head a fraction. In the moonlight, his bright green eyes were wide and afraid. 'Salib.'

'Salib who?'

'Just Salib.' John looked away.

'What did he want?'

'Nothing . . . Just for me to hook him up with any migrants looking for a way into Italy.'

Spike's chest suddenly felt tight. 'Did you hook Zahra up with Salib?'

'Zahra told me Dinah had a kid or something; she wanted to ask Salib some questions, check they were both OK.' He swept aside his blond fringe defensively. 'She knew the migrants were skipping to Italy as well as I did. I don't see why it's such a big deal.'

'Because she's missing, John.'

John glanced down at his wristwatch. 'Can I go now?'

'How many men did you send to Salib?' Spike said, stepping towards him. 'How many old people?'

John gave an amused snort.

'Because he only wanted the girls, right?' Spike shifted his weight from foot to foot. His joints felt lacquered now, his muscles sharp and precise. 'Did he tell you only to approach the pretty ones? Pay you a bonus if you cherry-picked a real beauty?'

John raised his eyes. This time he held Spike's gaze.

'Where did you send her, John?'

'Eat me.'

Slowly, Spike tilted back his head, then brought his brow crashing down on the bridge of John Petrovic's nose. There was a crack, like a fist crushing a walnut, followed by the reeling pain of having walked into a low-hanging beam.

Spike staggered backwards. When he opened his eyes, John was kneeling before him, blood pattering into the sand from between his cupped hands.

'Where did you send her, John?'

John groaned into his palms, rocking back and forth.

'*Where?*'

'Racecourse Street.' His voice was reedy and nasal.

'Where's Racecourse Street?'

'In Marsa. By the Sporting Club. That's all I know.'

Spike was already walking back towards the road.

8

The taxi drew to a halt. 'Here is Marsa.'

'I need Racecourse Street.'

'I told you, mister, I don't know any Racecourse Street.'

The cabbie kept his hands on the wheel, refusing to drive further. Spike paid what was on the meter and got out.

Half a mile earlier, they'd passed an industrial dockland, with the entrance to the original migrant camp opposite. After that they'd wound through the narrow streets of a residential working-class district: hardware stores, launderettes, rotting window frames contrasting with the ornate balconies of Valletta. The taxi had stopped at the mouth of a road, beside a wall with the words 'Marsa Sports Club' daubed in bull-blood red. Spike watched it reverse quickly away, then drive back in the direction of the docks.

He turned and headed along the wall. Poorly lit alleys sloped down to meet it; he checked the street names but they were all in Maltese.

A squat woman bustled towards him with a shopping bag. 'Racecourse Street?' Spike said, but she lowered her whiskered chin and increased her speed.

He took out the Mifsud address book and made a call. A female voice answered in Maltese.

'Natalya?' Spike said.

'Is Clara. You want speak Natalya?'

'Is Michael there?'

An old-fashioned click, then the Baron picked up. 'Home safe?'

'I decided to stay on for Carnival.'

'How wonderful.'

'I'm trying to look up an old friend. The trouble is, I have the street name in English but I need it in Maltese.'

'What is it in English?'

'Racecourse Street.'

There was a pause. The distant rev of a motorbike came from a passageway behind.

'Are you sure that's where your friend lives?'

'Yes.'

'It's just . . . I'm not sure it's a very good area.'

'I can look after myself, Michael. Now do you have the name?'

'Triq it-Tiġrija,' the Baron said in perfect Maltese. 'But I really don't –'

Spike thanked him and hung up.

9

Spike checked the name of each triq he passed. A barred gate appeared in the wall: he peered through and saw what looked like the concourse of a racetrack. He continued on until the street began to brighten. Lamp posts rose ahead on a crumbled-down pavement. Finally he saw a name painted in white along the top of the wall: 'Triq it-Tiġrija'.

A woman emerged from the shadows, whispering in Maltese. She wore red PVC trousers and a leather basque; judging by her height and jutting Adam's apple, she had not been a woman for long.

Two heavy-set men stood beneath a street light, each holding a birdcage in one hand. They fell silent as Spike approached. Their birds cocked their heads, each staring at Spike with tiny ink-spot eyes.

'I'm looking for Salib.'

One of the men raised his chin from a bed of neck fat and motioned up the street. Spike walked away, hearing the chaffinches chattering excitedly in their cages.

The street grew wider. Four women in stockings and bikini tops leaned against a parked car, overplucked eyebrows rippling like waves as Spike passed. He glanced into an alley and saw a girl in leopard-print leggings quietly unlocking a door.

A bar appeared on the pavement. Spike looked back at the men with their birdcages, and the same man motioned with a large hand towards it.

The bar had a row of plastic chairs with backs pressed to the facade. Two men occupied them, each with a birdcage at his feet. In Marsa, instead of walking a dog in the evening, apparently you walked the chaffinch.

Inside, an older man sat filling out a betting slip. The bar had a pinboard of currency notes behind it, beer on tap and a man rinsing pint glasses on a spray jet. Spike relaxed a little; this place would do OK in Gib.

He sat down on a stool. The barman rinsed another glass. He was tall and thin with a florid rash across his nose and cheeks.

'Pint of lager, please,' Spike said.

The barman cupped an ear, then brought his head closer. His breath smelled of pickled eggs. Spike pointed at the beer tap, and the man nodded, pulling a pint which was largely foam. Spike handed over a ten-euro note, which the barman slipped into the pocket of his cords before returning to washing glasses.

Spike rotated his stool. The man with the betting slip was gone. A white panel van rolled by outside. When Spike turned back to the bar, his pint had part liquefied; he took a sip and found it warm and flat. 'I'm looking for Salib,' he said.

The squirt of the drinks rinser wilted.

'Do you know him?'

The barman shook his head, then fired up the fountain again. Spike looked past him to a rear door. Voices outside: some kind of beer garden, perhaps.

'John Petrovic sent me.'

The barman swivelled his head. 'American John?'

'He told me to ask for Salib.'

A grin exposed a set of brown stumpy teeth. 'You like girlies?'

Spike gave a wink, and the barman approached, reaching into his back pocket. 'For friends of John,' he said, returning Spike's ten-euro note, 'is on the house.' His accent was heavily Maltese but the words were comprehensible.

Spike tucked the note back into his wallet, seeing a Gibraltar five-pound note inside, which he took out instead. 'For your collection.'

The barman smiled and pinned the note to the board behind. 'Come,' he said, motioning to the back door.

Beer garden had been overstating things: a collapsed outhouse formed a rubble-strewn rear courtyard. In the only clear corner, a plank of wood had been stretched over two upturned flowerpots. A family of three sat eating what looked like rabbit stew; the woman and her son stared at Spike, while the man kept his back turned, stabbing at a chunk of meat with a knife.

'Is better you go through,' the barman said, sensitively

indicating the child. He unlatched the gate in the wall. It gave onto a dusty track, with a broad single-storey building opposite.

'Wait here,' the barman said. 'Five minutes.'

10

Spike eased his way through the cockeyed gate. The building on the other side of the track housed a series of stables. The upper halves of the doors were open but the horses had the sense to be grazing elsewhere. The smell of manure and damp hay was sharp and pungent.

Adjoining the stables was an open-ended shack: tools, inner tyres, leather saddles on walls. Spike crouched down and found a smooth spar of wood loose on the ground.

From inside the beer garden came a click as the inner door closed: must be the family, going back into the bar.

The moon was almost full, casting a pale light on the dusty track. Spike stooped down further as the sound of an engine approached. A few seconds later, a motorcycle appeared. As it drew closer, Spike saw that its rider wore a black helmet. He gripped the handle of his cudgel more tightly.

The motorcycle stopped, the rider kicking down the footstand, then swinging his legs off the bike. The man's hands went to his head; as soon as Spike saw his helmet start to rise, he set off at a sprint towards him.

The man must have heard Spike approach, turning at the last moment, so that Spike's cudgel made contact with his temple rather than the back of his head. A smack of wood on bone echoed through the backstreet.

The man sank to his knees, helmet still gripped between his hands. Then he fell forward into the dust.

The man was lying face down, helmet just beyond his outstretched arms. Spike looked round: the motorcycle was parked a few yards behind. A throb of music pulsed from the street on the other side of the wall. The moon shone.

'Shit,' Spike said out loud.

He heaved the man onto his back. His lank dark hair receded to a widow's peak on a high forehead. His jaw was wide, an unexpected home for pink girlish lips, his blue canvas trousers fastened with what looked like fisherman's string. It was hard to tell if he was breathing or not.

Reaching forward, Spike held the back of his hand under the man's nose. A faint warmth tickled the skin. He patted him down, hoping to find a wallet. Nothing but a small set of padlock keys. Digging his hands beneath the man's muscled flanks, he rolled him onto his side, ready to check the back pockets. As the man turned over, his white T-shirt rucked up his back, revealing the base of a tattoo. Spike pushed the material higher and saw half of a Maltese cross, thickly inked.

Something moved in front: the man's hands were clasping the sides of his motorcycle helmet. Spike made a grab for the cudgel but the man was too quick, swivelling on one hip and swinging his helmet up with both arms so that it collided with Spike's forehead.

Spike stumbled backwards and fell heavily onto his coccyx. The man was already on his feet; he stepped to the left and kicked Spike neatly under the chin with the point of his toes. Spike felt his neck snap back and a sharp heat in his throat. Then he was lying on the ground, staring up at the moon, unable to hear anything except a swirling seashell sound in his ears.

Spike sensed a shadow move above. The noise in his ears had stopped; he realised he was still lying on the track, head tilted back in the dust, staring up at the night sky.

He tried to stand but his arms were jammed in the pockets of his trousers. He moved his eyes downwards and saw a rubber bicycle tyre squeezed around his hips.

The man reappeared. With his left hand, he swept his thin black hair into its peak. Then he reached down and picked up a plastic canister.

Spike tried to force his arms out but the tyre was too tight around his midriff. He kicked with his feet to push himself away. The rubber tread gripped the ground, holding him in place. His face was hot, sweat soaking his T-shirt.

The man stared down. One of his cheeks was shiny with blood.

'I have money,' Spike said. 'Five thousand euros.'

The man seemed to hesitate. Then he started unscrewing the lid of the canister.

'Ten thousand,' Spike said as the man dropped the cap onto the ground.

It was then that Spike started to shout. A moment later, his cries became retches as the man sloshed petrol into his face. His eyes burned, vomit mixing with saliva, heaving from the depths of his stomach, making him gag and convulse so much that he managed to flip over onto his side.

The man was walking away. Footsteps in the distance, the sound of a motorbike wheeled towards him. Spike's eyes were open but he could see nothing but a grey blur.

The rattle of a matchbox, a hissing Maltese voice. The slow slide of the box opening. The rasp of a match on the striking strip . . .

Imperceptibly, Spike's thoughts turned to Zahra, and he found himself less afraid. A flame glowed above, a halo of orange around it. He waited for the heat, for the shrieks to rise from his chest until the dizziness engulfed the agony. The match was burning, so brightly he realised he must already be alight, yet there was no pain. How clever, he thought, the body arranged it so there would be no pain. What a thing to discover so late.

He listened to the long, loud hoot of a horn. Shouting echoed, an exchange of voices. An engine revving, then a motorbike passing beside him, kicking up dust which caked the inside of his mouth.

Hands rolled him over. The glow came from car headlights, not a flame. The face above wore a small neat moustache.

'My boy,' whispered the Baron. 'My poor, dear boy.'

✳

She sits in the same position, legs out, back against the bars, chin lolling. Her upper arms throb: an infection spreading between the needle marks, joining the dots.

Deep within the cavern, the man's voice sounds agitated as he talks on a mobile phone. A word is spoken which jolts her from her fever. It reappears a few sentences later, the Maltese pronunciation rasping and harsh: *Geebraltah*.

She feels her cracked lips form a smile. Spike is here . . . he is looking for her.

The man stands, voice quieter as he issues what sounds like a warning down the phone. Then he turns, looking her way. She closes her eyes, dreading the footsteps. But instead comes the click of a padlock as the gate opens, then closes.

She raises her head. In the half-light, she sees new figures on the camp beds. Beside her, the same woman sits slumped. She has given up calling for her baby. Perhaps she is dead.

With added determination, she tries to force her arms away from the bars. The needle marks in her upper arms start to pound. Leaning to one side, she lets her right arm flop down, then stretches her hand as far from her body as it will go. Her fingers brush something: the rough weave of hemp. She has reached the ropes of the woman next to her. She digs her nails beneath the knot and starts to work it free.

Chapter Nine

I

Spike opened an eye. The wallpaper above was old and peeling, decorated with images of a stork carrying a baby bundle through the air. Sometimes the stork's wings were raised, sometimes lowered. The baby bundle remained the same.

Spike opened the other eye. He was stretched out on a metal-framed bed. Small, lace-trimmed pillows supported his head. A glass of water rested on the bedside table.

He sat up, shoulders throbbing. By the door, slumped in a wicker armchair, sat the Baroness. She wore white jeans and a sky-coloured linen shirt, her sandy hair tied back in a ponytail. In repose, her lips sagged as she breathed in and out.

Spike surveyed the bedroom, seeing his clothes washed and folded on the dresser, his espadrilles side by side below the cupboard. He blinked to clear the fog from his eyes, trying to remember the events of last night. Helped into the Baron's Daimler. A frantic drive back to Valletta. The cool sting of eye drops from the doctor's pipette. The unsympathetic tones of Clara as she'd reluctantly made up the spare room.

He moved his neck gingerly: the blow beneath his chin had bruised his windpipe. A taste of petrol lingered on his palate. Rainbows attached themselves to all sources of light. His retinas ached if they focused too long.

When he cleared his throat, the Baroness stirred, then got to her feet. 'How are you?' she whispered, coming over.

'Better. I think.'

She sat down on the edge of the bed. 'We were wondering whether to call your father.'

'Best not.'

She nodded. 'How are your eyes?'

'Not too bad.'

'That in Malta, little Malta . . .' She shook her head. 'Michael has already contacted the police. Given a description of the man. Apparently there've been robberies there before. Why did you go to Marsa?' she asked, suddenly angry. 'Sorry. You do not want to be interrogated. You go there for your own reasons. But Michael . . . when you phoned him, he worried and worried. Thank God he chose to go.'

'How did he find me?'

'He drove around. But you can ask him yourself, I'll send him up. If you're not too tired?'

Spike lay back. 'Maybe I'll just rest my eyes for a moment.' He was asleep before the Baroness had left the room.

2

Spike woke to a gentle sound of knocking. The glow from the curtains was a darker yellow: street lamps not sunshine. 'Yes?'

The door part opened to reveal the small upright figure of the Baron. 'Are you awake?' he hissed loudly.

'Yes.'

The Baron creaked towards him over the floorboards. His cords were a lurid red; from the collar of his checked shirt rose a spotted neckerchief. He gave an apologetic smile, then sat down awkwardly. Something about his presence in the half-light made

Spike fumble uneasily for the bedside lamp. It took a moment before a reassuring brightness illuminated the room.

'How are you, my boy?'

'Just relieved you found me. How did you know where to look?'

The Baron glanced over one shoulder. 'Don't tell Natalya,' he said, 'but I had a bit of a misspent youth. Went to Marsa a few times, if you know what I mean. The most notorious area was always by the stables. But I never heard of anything like that happening.'

'Do they know who he is?'

'Not yet. But they're looking for him.'

'He had a tattoo on his back,' Spike said. 'A Maltese cross. Did you tell them that?'

'Of course. The police are doing all they can, but don't expect miracles. This isn't Scotland Yard.'

Spike tried to climb out of bed, but the Baron put a hand on his chest. 'Your job is to get better. You let me deal with this, OK?'

3

Another knock at the door. This time the room streamed with natural light.

'*Visita*,' came Clara the maid's monotone.

Spike drew himself up into a sitting position, noting that the pain in his shoulders had diminished.

Rachel Cassar appeared in the doorway. She covered her mouth in shock as she crossed the room.

'Do I look that bad?'

'Are you sure you're up for visitors?'

'It's fine. Good to have the company.'

She was about to sit down on the bed, then thought better of it, choosing the wicker armchair instead. 'Does it hurt?'

'I've had worse.'

'In *Gib*?' she said, trying to be playful. Quickly defeated, she looked around, taking in the nursery-themed decor. 'Why did they put you in here?'

Spike rubbed the sheets, which gave off a plastic crinkle. 'I was throwing up when I arrived. Safest place.'

'Bit creepy, if you ask me. The child that never was.'

There was a pause as they stared at each other, minds moving uncomfortably to the night before last.

'How did you know I was still in Malta?'

Rachel looked away. 'The message you left about David's studio . . . I called the Baron in case he knew more about it. He was David's landlord, after all.' She glanced round to the door. 'He told me what had happened. Do you still have keys to the studio, by the way?' she asked, looking back.

'I gave them back to the estate agent.'

'Already?'

'It was just a poky room. I cleared it out myself. The contents are all downstairs in the flat. Why does it matter?'

A creak came from outside the door. 'Better to talk later,' Rachel whispered. 'When are you fit to leave?'

'The doctor's coming at lunchtime. After that, I suppose.'

'I could meet you tonight at the flat? Eight o'clock?'

'If you like.'

Rachel got to her feet. 'Marsa, eh?'

'It's not what you think.'

'When the knights first came to Malta, the Grand Master tried to close down the brothels. There were full-scale riots from the locals. Prostitution has been legal ever since.'

Spike didn't have the energy to argue back. Rachel reached for the door handle, then turned again. 'You could just have given me a call,' she said with a wink.

Once she'd gone, Spike lay back heavily on the pillows, hearing distant voices downstairs. The lights were still surrounded by a strange, iridescent fog; he rubbed his eyeballs, then swept an arm beneath the bed for his phone. As soon as it switched on, it burst into life with a message from Azzopardi, his tone urgent, serious. Hearing the word 'Zahra', Spike sat up, finishing the message before swinging his legs out of bed.

Another creak as the Baroness peered round the door. 'What are you doing?' she asked.

'Got to go.'

'Where to?'

'The hospital.'

'We can take you.'

'It's not about me.'

He pulled on his jumper, then pecked at the Baroness's withered cheek, catching a scent of stale vodka beneath the rosewater. 'Thanks for helping,' he said. 'Sorry.'

4

The Mater Dei Hospital was a modern, low-slung building, sprawling over an area of wasteland just off the bypass outside Valletta. The taxi stopped in the car park. The hospital's facade looked as though it had recently been touched up with a flesh-coloured coat of render.

'Get well soon,' the cabbie said, assessing Spike's appearance in the rear-view mirror.

Spike slammed the back door, then walked through the car park. A blonde woman was penguin-waddling through the main entrance, hands on an enormous baby-bump as a lanky, anxious man trailed behind. Spike followed them into the reception area.

Azzopardi was sitting on one of a rank of moulded chairs, legs crossed elegantly, talking to a member of his Mobile Squad. The moment he saw Spike, he rose from his seat.

The usual confident smile was missing. Spike felt his windpipe throb as Azzopardi gave a small but unmistakable shake of the head.

Spike closed his eyes; it felt as though the floor were tipping. When he opened them, Azzopardi was standing beside him. He placed an arm on his shoulder and steered him towards the plastic seats.

Spike sat down, brow resting on fists. A crunching echoed through his skull: he was scratching his knuckles back and forth against his scalp. A numbness started to take over, strangely familiar. 'OK,' he said, looking back up. 'Let's get this done.'

5

Spike followed Azzopardi down a long strip-lit corridor. The rubber soles of Azzopardi's colleague squeaked behind them on the linoleum; he tried to lighten his tread, but the squeaking continued. Round the corner, a horizontal sign dangled from a chain: 'Mortuary'. A cloying reek of formaldehyde sweetened the air. 'OK?' Azzopardi said.

Spike nodded; Azzopardi knocked on a door and they went inside.

The room gleamed: porcelain tiles, stainless-steel tables, walls covered with what looked like rows of school lockers, minus the stickers and graffiti. In one corner, a middle-aged man stood beside a gurney. He wore blue scrubs and round wire-rimmed glasses. He nodded at Azzopardi, then started to wheel the gurney to the far wall. The wing of a dicky bow rose above his collar.

'Forensic pathologist,' Azzopardi said. 'Also called Mifsud, incidentally,' he added, then seemed to regret it.

The pathologist rotated the handle of one of the lockers, then drew out a stainless-steel tray. The corpse was covered by a white shroud. At one end, Spike made out the oval shape of a face, at the other, the upturned points of toes. He felt his Adam's apple slide up and down his throat.

The pathologist snapped on a pair of latex gloves. He glanced again at Azzopardi, who turned to Spike. 'You want to take a moment?'

'No. Do it now.'

The pathologist moved to the end of the gurney, and a stiff coffee-coloured arm flopped out of the shroud, a web of needle marks defacing its inner side. With blank recognition, Spike took in the smooth skin, the unpainted nails. The shroud edged backwards, exposing Zahra's beautiful almond-shaped eyes, closed as though in sleep. Her lips were pale, blue-tinged and less full somehow, her hair long and tangled, massed in curls around her neck . . .

'It's not her.'

All eyes turned to Spike, but he continued to stare at the girl's face. 'It looks like her, but it's not.'

Azzopardi seemed to be searching Spike's expression for evidence of hysteria.

'It's not Zahra,' he repeated.

In response to a signal from Azzopardi, the pathologist drew the shroud back further, revealing the girl's long, elegant neck and heavy breasts. The areolas were broad and brown.

'Are you sure?'

'One hundred per cent.'

The pathologist said something in Maltese. 'Any distinguishing features?' Azzopardi asked.

'On the small of her back,' Spike replied. 'Two dimples. They're quite pronounced.'

The pathologist pushed the errant arm back beneath the sheet, then put his hands on the girl's hip, rolling her over. The back of the girl's head had been smashed to a clotted, hairy pulp. Two welts lay beneath each shoulder blade; otherwise, the rest of her upper back was unblemished, the skin so smooth, Spike thought as the shroud continued to creep down, that perhaps it was Zahra, and his earlier response really had been one of denial. He felt his bowels shift as the shroud kept lowering. The raised zip-line of vertebrae; the top of the girl's buttocks. No dimples on the small of her back.

'You see,' Spike said.

The pathologist re-covered the corpse. Spike felt the dizziness returning; he reached out and found his hand clutching the frame of the gurney. A moment later he was outside in the corridor, sitting with his head between his knees. It felt as though he'd somehow been given a reprieve.

The door opened and Azzopardi emerged.

'I know who she is,' Spike said, looking up.

6

Spike sat with Azzopardi in the front of an unmarked Alfa Romeo, his colleague behind, bored in the back seat. An orange windsock fluttered above the car-park wall, marking a helipad for the hospital air ambulance.

Azzopardi's radio gave a crackle; he reached forward and turned it off. In the alcove by the gearstick lay a detachable blue light.

'I need a coffee,' Azzopardi said to Spike. 'Want one?' Without awaiting an answer, he leaned back and spoke to his colleague. Exuding an air of resignation, the colleague got out and set off across the car park.

'I owe you an apology,' Azzopardi said. A lock of his slicked-back hair had worked itself free, hanging over his brow like a snapped antenna. He trained it back. 'So who is she?'

'A Somali. She's called Dinah; Dinah Kassim, I think. She disappeared from the Hal Far migrant camp three weeks ago.'

Azzopardi drew a Moleskine notebook from his glove compartment. 'And your friend is still missing?'

'Zahra al-Mahmoud.' Spike spelled out the name, waiting for Azzopardi to write it down.

'And she looks like the dead woman?'

'Didn't her flatmate give you a photograph?'

Azzopardi shrugged. 'The duty sergeant dealt with it.'

Spike bit back his irritation, then reached for his wallet. The photograph dated from last year in Tangiers. Somehow he'd never quite been able to throw it away.

'*Haqq Alla*,' Azzopardi swore, tucking the picture into his notebook. 'They do look alike.'

'Her hair's shorter now.'

'I remember; she's very beautiful.'

'Yes.'

'So you think that Zahra's disappearance is linked to what happened to Dinah?'

'No question.' Spike told Azzopardi of his latest trip to the camps – the tip-off about John Petrovic and the underage girls, his involvement with people smuggling. 'John sent Zahra to meet a man called Salib. Heard of him?'

Spike thought he saw a shadow move across Azzopardi's face. 'No.'

'I went to try and find him in Marsa.'

'Is that where you lost your looks?'

'What?' Spike was confused for a moment, then touched his nose. 'Oh, right. Yes.'

'You met him then. This "Salib".'

'He tried to burn me alive.'

Azzopardi stopped writing, and Spike explained what had happened outside the stables. 'I think he's the same guy who's been following me since I arrived in Valletta. He'd have killed me last night if the Baron hadn't turned up.'

'The Baron?'

'Michael Malaspina. An old friend of my uncle's. I asked him for directions to Racecourse Street, and he got worried. Came and found me in his Daimler.'

Azzopardi added this name to his notebook.

'Didn't the Baron tell you this?'

'If so, it hasn't filtered up the food chain yet. Did you get a look at your attacker?'

'Black hair, high forehead. Long, pale face. And a tattoo on his back. A Maltese cross.'

'That explains the nickname, then.'

'Sorry?'

'*Is-Salib*. It means "the Cross" in Maltese. Did you get his bike registration?'

'Too dark.'

The windsock hung limply above the car-park wall; a moment later it leapt into life, like an idle worker interrupted.

'How did Dinah die?' Spike said.

Azzopardi closed his jotter. 'She ran out into the road last night. Half naked, jacked up on something strong. The bus driver didn't see her in time. The case wouldn't normally have made it to the Mobile Squad, except . . .'

'Except what?' Spike asked, dreading the answer.

'The pathologist found evidence of serious sexual assault – bruising and tears around the anus and vagina.'

'Any DNA?'

'Her rapist or rapists used condoms.'

They sat for a moment in silence.

'I assume we're looking at people trafficking here,' Spike said.

'What makes you say that?'

'A vulnerable woman. Drugged. Raped . . .'

Azzopardi made a series of soft clicking noises with his tongue. 'I'd have to think long and hard about that. The normal trafficking scenario involves girls being blackmailed or tricked into travelling overseas. They're sold on to a network of pimps and forced into off-street prostitution – saunas, massage parlours, that kind of thing. It's organised crime, Spike. Not something we get much of in Malta.'

'You don't run into a road half naked unless you're trying to escape someone or something. Was her baby with her?'

'Still unaccounted for.'

'And the bus hit her in Marsa, right?' Spike said.

'Just outside. On the road above the harbour.'

'Then we need to start looking there.'

Azzopardi gave a nod, then turned on the engine.

7

Though his eyes still hurt, Spike was starting to feel almost human as he passed once again beneath the City Gate. The police artist had not been without talent, and Azzopardi had already circulated an e-fit of Salib among the regional police stations of Malta and Gozo. He'd also sent one of his team to St Julian's to pick up John Petrovic for questioning. In the minds of the police, Zahra's disappearance was now linked to a murder investigation. And that meant that for the first time since arriving in Malta, Spike had some help.

Spike checked the time: 6 p.m. Valletta ought to be deserted by now but Republic Street was thick with people. A distant sound of drums and pipes came from up ahead; he skirted the edge of the crowd and saw a formation of schoolboys in the middle of St

George's Square. One line wore red tunics with a white cross on the front; they carried shields and wooden broadswords, beaming delightedly beneath their silver-painted helmets. The opposite line wore yellow turbans with rolled-up hems; their swords were curved, identifying them as Ottoman Turks. A bizarre Carnival re-enactment of the Great Siege, Spike decided as he turned onto Triq Sant'Orsla.

The South American music seller was doing a decent trade, having relocated his stall to the street corner. He gave Spike a nod as he passed.

His phone was ringing; he stopped beside a red British pillar box.

'We've found a possible safe house,' Azzopardi said. 'Want to tag along? We might need you to identify Salib.'

Spike put out an arm to the pillar box, suddenly light-headed again. 'Pick me up outside the cathedral.'

8

It was dark when the Transit van stopped on the road above the sea wall. Spike, Azzopardi and five members of his Mobile Squad got out, setting off down the steps which zigzagged down the inside of the wall. Spike's flak jacket felt too tight across his chest; as he started to tug down the zip, one of Azzopardi's colleagues spun round, putting a finger to his mouth.

They reached the marina at the bottom of the steps. Bobbing on the jetties was a ragbag of boats: trawlers, sailing boats, dinghies. Though they lacked the gaudy colours of the fishing boats of Marsaxlokk, Spike could still see their Eyes of Osiris glowing eerily in the moonlight, as slanted and delicate in shape as Zahra's.

A concrete walkway stretched ahead, sloping up from the foul-smelling water to a row of warehouses and storage areas sunk into the fortified wall behind. Spike passed the first and peered inside. A barred gate protected a deep, cavernous space: he made out the muzzle of what looked like a dragon, casting a macabre shadow on the ground below. Carnival floats, Azzopardi had said: a boy who'd been resurrecting one for this year's event had heard disturbing noises from a neighbouring warehouse, and made a report of possible squatters.

Azzopardi pinned himself to the wall between the last two warehouses. His colleagues did the same, and Spike followed, feeling the unsteadiness return to his legs as he thought again of Dinah lying on the slab. When he leaned forward, he saw Azzopardi motion to his nearest colleague. The man held a pair of bolt cutters, which Azzopardi took, clamping the jaws around the padlock and snapping them shut. A moment later, he and his men were ripping the iron gates apart.

A light had been turned on inside, a single naked bulb illuminating the space. As Spike passed between the gates, he was hit by a smell of raw sewage. Ranged on either edge of the warehouse were a series of camp beds; Azzopardi was crouching beside one, pulling back the blanket. Spike saw a small head appear. As Azzopardi placed his fingers on the figure's neck, the blanket fell away, revealing a naked girl lying on her front. From her scrawny, half-grown shape, Spike knew it was not Zahra. Her dark brown shoulder blades jutted; the skin on her arms was dotted with trackmarks. Azzopardi turned her chin; some kind of discharge oozed from her mouth. She gave a cough, and Azzopardi shouted, '*Ambulanza*,' to one of his colleagues, who ran outside, radio in hand.

Spike picked up the blanket and laid it over the girl, feeling his stomach turn as she shrank from his touch. The adjacent bed was empty. In front, another member of the Mobile Squad was crouching by a young West African, who lashed out with her arms as he tried to calm her.

Spike's eyes began to adjust, and he counted over twenty beds, four occupied by girls in varying states of distress. He walked down the central aisle, seeing a child's paddling pool half filled in one corner, a drain clogged with faeces, a fridge-freezer with a kettle on top.

More shouts; Spike glanced round, then continued into the darkest recess of the warehouse. The rear wall had two arched metal gates in the brickwork, ropes coiled around the bars, as though animals had been tethered there. He pressed his face to the grilles and saw rolls of rotting orange fishing nets behind.

He looked back round. One of the Mobile Squad was leaning a palm against the side of the kettle, testing for heat in the same way Azzopardi had felt for the girl's pulse. He lowered his hand then opened the fridge door. A light winked on inside.

Spike saw a frown form on the man's brow. One hand held the fridge door, while the other moved to his chest. He was crossing himself.

Spike stepped behind the man and stared into the fridge. The baby boy was wedged side-on in the ice compartment. His tiny body was swaddled in oilskin rags, but the face was visible, eyes wide, staring out as if in surprise. The frosted commas of his eyebrows contrasted with the darker skin of his cheeks. The irises seemed to have leaked into the whites, discolouring their surfaces, which had ruptured in the freezing cold, crystallising as though dusted with brown sugar.

The policeman bent over and retched. Spike reached forward and closed the fridge door.

Sitting on the concrete dock on the other side of the police cordon, Spike saw onlookers peering down, drawn by the silent, rotating lights of the water ambulance which was now moored in the marina.

In the flashing lights, he made out the sides of the boats on the nearest jetty. Most seemed to be pleasure vessels, but one looked more industrial, with a broader, deeper hull: *Calypso Lines*. The second jetty was illuminated by police floodlights: just one large boat, *Falcon Freight*. Spike typed both names into his mobile phone, then saw Azzopardi coming towards him over the walkway.

Azzopardi nodded at the boats. 'Don't worry. We'll be searching them one by one.' He ducked beneath the cordon and handed Spike a paper cup.

The water ambulance gave a brief, solitary wail, as Spike put the cup to his mouth and sucked out the tepid coffee. He hoped it had not been made with water from the kettle in the warehouse.

'My father's on his way,' Azzopardi said. Spike saw an officer on the other side of the cordon raise an eyebrow at a colleague, then turn his back.

'Are the girls going to be OK?' Spike asked.

'We don't know.'

Two female paramedics emerged from the warehouse. The black Ziploc bag on the stretcher between them was flat save for a small, raised bump in the middle. Spike felt his throat thicken as the ambulance engine started, propeller blades churning the oily water.

'Do you want me to find you a lift back to town?' Azzopardi said.

'I'd appreciate it.'

'We're going to keep this out of the press. No call to upset the tourists during Carnival. But we'll be looking for her, Spike. All leave is cancelled. Coastguards, traffic units. Everyone's mobilised.'

Spike watched Azzopardi duck again beneath the cordon, then walk away along the line of warehouses. His mobile was ringing: Rachel Cassar. He cut her off, then stared out in silence at the dark Mediterranean sea.

✳

The ground is rocking. Only when the ground is still can she think. The others seem to suffer too, as she hears a small scared groan in the darkness. '*Belesh*,' she calls out in Arabic. *It will stop*.

Her prediction is right. The floor steadies and the breathing around her grows regular. Following her nightly ritual, she closes her eyes, forcing the images into her mind like slides into a projector.

Her father, cross-armed outside their front door, orange sand dunes rising behind, grinning lopsidedly as the tail of his blue turban flutters in the desert wind. Then the only photograph she ever saw of her mother, sitting on a kilim carpet, kneading the wheat flour and water, younger then than she herself is now, bright eyes gazing up, puzzled as to why anyone would wish to point a camera at her. Then later, in Tangiers, the daughter of the shopkeeper who would throw her arms around her neck, squeezing so tightly that she could hardly breathe, showing off her finger paintings, hugging her close. How gentle Spike's eyes look even when his voice is rough, how she would teach him to trust again, to love. She imagines them sitting together on a balcony, looking out over the Strait of Gibraltar, at the waves changing direction as the currents shift, white horses rearing in the blue, seabirds soaring, Africa in the background, steadying somehow, she reading, he watching her read, she kneading bread, he with his arms crossed, standing outside the house they would eventually buy, a little girl squeezing her neck, their little girl, with his gentle eyes as she smiles upwards, wondering why anyone would choose now of all moments to take a photograph . . .

Tears spill. Her mind blurs as the ground starts to rock again. Footsteps above, men climbing aboard . . .

Spike won't give up, she tells herself. He will come for her. He won't give up.

Chapter Ten

I

Spike opened his eyes. At first he thought he was back in the Baron's palazzo, then he saw light seeping in through the plywood window. The Mifsud flat: he'd crashed out fully clothed on his uncle and aunt's bed.

He stared up at the ceiling as a creak came from above: the Baron and Baroness, starting a new day. His head ached; realising how thirsty he was, he rolled out of bed and checked the cupboards in the kitchen. Two untouched bottles of rum; he took one down, unscrewed the cap and poured out three fingers. The burn on his tongue reignited the taste of petrol, but he swallowed it down, then filled the glass from the tap and drank greedily. The next cupboard was lined with tinned food. He grabbed some tuna and tomatoes, opened the fridge, then stopped. The sight of the ice compartment made his stomach lurch. Appetite gone, he returned to the bedroom.

One voicemail from Galliano; he ignored it and punched in the number for Drew Stanford-Trench.

'Welcome back, pal.'

'I'm still in Malta.'

'How come?'

'It's the new Ibiza. Listen, Drew, can you do me a favour?'

'You name it.'

'That Internet site you subscribed to. For the Harrington case.'

'Yachtfinder.com.'

'Do you still have access?'

'Sadly yes. The minimum subscription was for a year.'

'Does it only list yachts? Or does it keep details of commercial vessels?'

'Anything over a certain footage.'

'Can you take down some names for me?' Spike heard a rustle of what sounded like bedclothes.

'Fire away.'

'One is *Falcon Freight*, the other, *Calypso Lines*.'

'What am I looking for?'

'Ownership predominantly – but I'd be interested in anything irregular. Use your initiative.'

'I'm on my way to the office now. Can I call you from there?'

Spike checked the time: 11 a.m. 'Sure,' he chuckled. The sound was unfamiliar. 'Sorry to interrupt, Drew. And thanks for your help.'

'Bring me back some Maltesers and we'll call it quits.'

Spike's appetite was returning; he opened up the cans of tuna and tomatoes and mashed them together in a white china bowl. Sitting at the kitchen table, he spooned the combination into his mouth, trying to focus his mind enough to think.

A rap came from the door; still carrying the bowl, Spike went to the hallway and slid all three bolts firmly in place.

'My darlink?' came a voice from behind the door.

He drew back the bolts and found the Baron and Baroness standing outside. They peered in like a couple of well-heeled Jehovah's witnesses.

'You went to the hospital?' the Baroness asked.

Spike swallowed his mouthful of tuna. 'And all's well.'

'Is it?' the Baroness said pointedly. Her powdered brow was crinkled. 'Michael and I have been talking,' she said in a gentler voice. 'You've had a shock. You must go home to your father.'

'Just a few more days.'

'Why?'

Spike glanced from her to the Baron, who was smiling conspiratorially. 'I'm still trying to track down my friend.'

'That was why you were in Marsa?' the Baroness said.

Spike nodded.

'Perhaps we can help. We know many people.'

'It's fine. Really.'

'How about supper?' the Baron said, looking down into Spike's bowl. 'Get some proper grub into you.'

'That'd be great. But I'm going to rest for now.'

The Baroness set off back towards the palazzo, while the Baron lingered, sniffing the air, moustache twitching as he caught the rum on Spike's breath. 'That girl was back here last night,' he said.

'Which girl?' Spike replied at once.

'The curvy one. From the museum. She spent a while knocking on your door.'

Spike exhaled. 'I missed an appointment with her.'

'I'll say,' the Baron added with a wink. 'Beats the hell out of a trip to Marsa.'

'Michael?' came the Baroness's shrill voice from round the corner.

The Baron rolled his eyes. 'See you later,' he said, '8 p.m. as per. We can head out to Carnival afterwards. Have a gawp at the dancers.' With a knowing grin, he set off in the direction of his wife.

Back in the kitchen, Spike discarded his half-eaten food, then brought up Azzopardi's number on his phone.

2

Azzopardi answered immediately. His voice was hushed, as though speaking in a library.

'Where are you?' Spike asked.

'At the hospital.'

'Are the girls OK?'

'They were all drugged with the same mix of codeine and heroin. All showed signs of sexual assault. But they'll live.'

'And the baby? Was it Dinah's?'

'The lab's working on it.'

Spike heard a squeak of linoleum. 'Why kill a child?'

'Probably an accident. Or he got in the way.'

'Any other leads?'

'One set of prints from the safe house. We're working our contacts in the camps but it's hard to get information from the migrant community. My Mobile Squad are going door to door in Marsa, but as you can imagine, the locals are none too welcoming.'

'How about the marina?'

'It's more of a scrapyard. The boats were all empty. Nothing.'

'Petrovic?'

'Left the country the morning after your altercation. Plane to London then Atlanta. I don't hold out much hope of extradition.' Spike heard muffled chatter in the background; Azzopardi responded in Maltese, then spoke again to Spike. 'The youngest girl has woken up. We're waiting for the doctor to confirm she's fit for questioning.'

'You'll ask her about Zahra?'

'My opening line.'

Spike sensed Azzopardi preparing to hang up. 'What's your gut instinct on this?' he said.

The squeaking linoleum fell silent. 'We think this "Salib" may be Sicilian. He brings a boat over twice a year, picks up migrants from the warehouse. It starts off as people smuggling, then he gets greedy, takes to drugging the girls and selling them to the Mafia.'

'A Sicilian with a tattoo of a Maltese cross?'

'Maybe it's a celebration of how he earns his living. A tribute to our national symbol.'

Spike let that pass. 'He can't have been working alone.'

'Probably not.'

'So you're saying he's back in Sicily? Taken Zahra with him?'

'We're liaising with the Italian police. But it's tricky these days; people can move between EU countries without even showing a passport.'

'She can't have just *vanished*.'

'Hold tight and I'll keep you posted.'

The picture hooks resembled insects climbing the bare walls. Finding his glass empty, Spike threw it into the grate, where it shattered, pieces scattering over the floorboards. From outside came the beat of Carnival. Another, lighter knock in the hallway. 'What am I, a fucking butler?' Spike swore to himself as he crossed the room and pulled open the door.

3

Rachel Cassar was waiting outside the flat. She wore the same silk shirt as in the cathedral, but her wavy hair was unwashed, loosely held in a ponytail. Her arms were folded across her chest, her eyes wide and expectant behind her black-rimmed specs. Slung over one shoulder was a computer case. 'Aren't you going to ask me in?' she said, before shaking her head and striding past him into the hallway.

Spike stared out at the empty street, seeing the statue of the apostle opposite in its corner niche. The fingers raised in the sign of the cross no longer seemed a blessing, but a gesture of aggression, or a curse. He turned back to the flat.

Rachel was in the sitting room now, eyes ranging over the walls.

'You OK?' Spike said.

'Very much so. You?' Her eyes dropped to the shattered pieces of his tumbler.

'If this is about last night, I'm sorry, something came up.'

She put down her laptop, then bent to one of the crates.

'What are you looking for, Rachel?'

'David's copy of the painting.'

'Why?'

'Because,' she said, 'I found pentimenti.'

'Regrets?'

Rachel moved to the next crate. 'Your father mentioned you spoke Italian. No, "regrets" is the literal meaning. I can assure you, there's nothing to feel bad about here.'

Spike watched her pick up her computer case, then settle in the chair beside the desk. Irritation began to flare through him like indigestion.

'Those photographs David took,' Rachel said, parting her laptop. 'I digitised the infrared images, and the computer slotted them together.'

Spike moved behind her and stared down at the screen. The attachment she'd opened showed a washed-out, negative version of the painting in Mifsud's original photograph. On closer examination, Spike saw it was composed of a mosaic of thirty or so images, formed of the blurred IR photographs Mifsud had taken. The white squares dotted within presumably represented the ones Spike had lost to the St James Ditch.

'A "pentimento" occurs when an artist starts to paint something one way, then regrets it and decides to paint over. See there?' Rachel pointed at a greyish blur to the right of the jailer's breeches. 'That's the start of a new figure. You can even see the shoes. An assistant to the jailer, I'd imagine. We'd have known more about him if you hadn't lost the rest of the photographs.'

'Why does this matter, Rachel?'

'Because,' she said, exasperation creeping into her voice, 'it suggests that the Gozo St Agatha is not a copy.'

Spike waited for this revelation to hit home.

'If someone is copying a painting,' Rachel went on, 'they'll make minor adjustments as they go. Human error. But major structural changes, like adding a figure, then choosing to take it out – that only tends to occur with original paintings.'

'And why is this significant?'

Rachel paused, as though unsure whether to continue. 'I think I mentioned before that there are lots of St Agathas in Malta.'

'You did.'

'Well, from the seventeenth century onwards, they all follow a similar structure and style. Because of this, most people believe that they were copied from a single original painting, now lost. A few eccentric academics even think this original was painted by Caravaggio. Do you follow?'

'Just about.'

'This is because they all share certain Caravaggian tropes.' She hit a key on the computer and the screen switched to Mifsud's basic photograph of the painting. 'See ... no putti beckoning Agatha up to heaven, no haloes, no sudden apparition of St Peter – just harsh, brutal naturalism. And there ... Agatha's hair, for example, is a swarthy Sicilian brown, rather than the usual angelic blonde. Then there's the fact that so few paintings are accounted for from Caravaggio's time on Malta. He was employed by the Order of St John for almost two years, he was a famously fast worker, so where are the fruits of his labours? The two masterpieces in the oratory, then four others abroad. But that's it. So a certain number of other paintings must be lost, the experts claim. Plundered by Napoleon. Squirrelled overseas. Or hanging misattributed in dingy chapels.'

'You sound dubious.'

'Caravaggio's influence in Malta was pervasive. With the St Agatha cycle ... a talented local artist could just have executed an original painting in the Caravaggian style, then had others copy it. There's no reason for the source material to have been by Caravaggio.'

'So that's what you're saying the Gozo St Agatha is? An original painting by a talented local artist?'

'That's what I assumed when I saw the first pentimento. But then something else struck me. I told you before about preliminary sketches.'

'Pencil lines?'

'The infrared picks up most strongly on those because the carbon content is highest.' Rachel switched the computer screen back to the IR photo-mosaic. 'Do you see any clear lines in this image?'

'It's too blurred.'

'Exactly,' Rachel declared with satisfaction. 'An ordinary artist creating a new painting would sketch out what he was going to paint first. In the baroque era, there was only one person skilful enough to forgo that process yet still produce a work like this.'

'Your man?'

'Michelangelo Merisi himself. Caravaggio didn't bother with anything as tedious as preliminary sketches; he just painted directly on the canvas. And not just any old canvas.' Rachel's fingers flitted around the image. 'Looks pale, doesn't it? That's because the canvas has been covered in a red underwash. That's another of Caravaggio's indicators: he used to wash his canvases with a red preparation, let them dry, then get started. The colour red is barely picked up by IR radiation. That's why the background looks so muted.' Rachel ran her hands through her hair; her ponytail came loose, the elastic tie falling to the ground.

'So you're suggesting David might have uncovered a lost Caravaggio?'

'I'm saying . . . I need to see the original.' She zipped the laptop back in its case.

'Good for David,' Spike said.

She sprang to her feet. 'Good for David? Is that all you can say? Do you have any concept of how few confirmed Caravaggios there are in existence? This would be like winning the lottery of the century.'

'But David wouldn't have gained financially. Surely the Church would own the painting. Or the Maltese government?'

'Forget ownership. Think of the status. Book tours. Lecture circuits. The respect and envy of your peers.' Her eyes glowed behind her spectacles.

'So where is the original?'

She dipped into another crate. 'Well, it's not in the chapel, I can tell you that. I've checked with the Gozo Curia and David didn't lodge any formal requests to remove it. So I started to wonder if someone else might have taken it. But then you told me about the copy David had been making.'

'I don't see why it's of such interest.'

'Because,' Rachel retorted, 'it means that David took the painting from the chapel himself.'

'No it doesn't.'

Rachel gave a contemptuous snort.

'David could have been painting his copy from a photograph.'

'But *you* picked those photographs up, don't you see? *After* David died. So he didn't have them with him. He must have been painting his copy from the original. And now *I* can't find it . . .'

After watching her scrabble through another crate, Spike turned and went to the kitchen, digging into the cardboard box he'd brought back from David's studio and carrying his half-finished copy into the sitting room. As soon as Rachel saw it, she swept Teresa's charity leaflets off the table. 'On there,' she ordered. 'No. There.'

Spike laid out the taut oval stretcher, feeling the last flickers of attraction extinguish. 'The heightened colours,' Rachel said with a gasp. 'It's as though David were painting a clean copy. To return to the chapel. To buy himself time . . .' She caressed the air above the canvas. Pencil lines showed where Mifsud had made his own preliminary sketches.

'How did David find out about the painting?'

Her hand stopped above the brightly bleeding torso of St Agatha. 'He spent a year going in and out of the Notarial Archives while working for me. He could have spotted an old inventory. A suggestion that the Gozo painting was misattributed.'

'Who's the original supposed to be by?'

'Some local nonentity called Lorenzo da Gozo. Worth, I don't know, seven hundred euros? As opposed to seventy *million*.' She glanced up. 'Are you sure this was the only painting left in the studio?'

'It was a broom cupboard, Rachel. I could barely squeeze in there myself.'

'Then David must have hidden the original. Put it in storage . . .'

'Or taken a snap on his camera phone and used that to make the copy.'

Rachel grabbed the stretcher and marched into the hallway. Spike heard her laptop case slip from her shoulder as she tried to open the door; when he came out to assist, she turned, pressed her lips to his, then exited into the early evening.

4

Spike remained in the doorway, staring out at the street. When he turned back to the flat, he caught sight of his reflection in the hallway mirror, three dark days of beard covering his cheeks.

He poured himself another slug of rum, then sat down at the kitchen table, pondering the bizarre nature of Rachel's visit. The light was fading at the window, another day slipping away. Hold tight, Azzopardi had said, but how would that help Zahra?

Azzopardi picked up at once. 'Are you still in Valletta?'

'Of course.'

'I'm sending some people to see you.'

'Have you found her?'

'No, but there've been developments.'

'You've arrested Salib?'

'Not yet. But forensics have made some interesting discoveries.'
It sounded as though he were getting into a car.

'Such as?'

'The prints from the warehouse. There's a match with the chapel in Gozo. We lifted one from the inside of the door.'

Spike said nothing.

'There's more. The spermicide found in the post-mortem on your aunt's body. It was the same as was used by Dinah's assailant.'

'An unusual kind?'

'From a particular brand of condom. I'm sending a team to the Mifsud flat to dust for prints. Can you go there and let them in?'

'I'm here now.'

'You're *what*?'

'I'm staying at the flat; you told me the case was closed, remember?'

Azzopardi cursed in Maltese. 'Well, don't touch anything. They'll be with you in fifteen minutes.'

Spike hung up. So Salib had been in Gozo . . . Looking for the painting, presumably – maybe he'd even murdered the priest to get hold of it. First you traffic women, then images of women – there was always a profit to be made from beauty. But could a man like Salib really have identified a misattributed Caravaggio? Mifsud must have spoken to someone about his discovery, let something slip, then word had filtered down to the underworld. Had Salib broken into the flat? Raped Teresa in order to find out the location of the painting . . .

Spike's phone was ringing.

'Spike?'

'Rachel? I can barely hear you.'
'Are you following me?'
'No. Why?'
The line went dead. Spike called her back: straight to voice-mail. He started composing a text, then stopped and ran out into the night.

5

The lion was rearing on its back legs, its fur a fluorescent yellow, its jaws crowded with papier-mâché teeth. Dancers in grass skirts clapped and stamped to the beat of a hidden boom box whining about the mighty jungle. Following behind was a unicorn, its horn coiled with silver foil. Men and women dressed as playing cards whirled around it, grim-faced, the rectangular cardboard stuck to their backs a burden restricting their movement.

Spike started crossing the street, but the next float was passing, a seagull with ink-spot eyes, its neck straddled by baby-oiled women with diaphanous wings sprouting from their shoulders. A group of men in glittery wigs bustled by, each clasping a toddler's hand, one of whom carried a streamer she kept trying to blow as her father dragged her along.

Spike heard a voice – 'Happy Carnival!' – and turned to see the Mifsud family lawyer chewing on a toffee apple, flanked by an effete man in a phallic Venetian mask. He gave them a nod, then pushed between the floats.

A girl dressed as a mermaid was taking a cigarette break on the other side of the road. She threw Spike a smile as he cast about for familiar street signs, seeing only the incomprehensible 'Triq San Patrizju'. Triq or treat . . . Picking up speed, he tried to visu-alise the city grid in his mind, instinctively veering east until finally he saw the Museum of Fine Arts. A few moments later he was outside Rachel's flat.

The lights were on upstairs, the Skoda parked outside. 'Rachel?' he called up to her balcony, but the music drowned out his voice. He depressed her buzzer, then the others, waiting until an elderly voice spoke back.

'Delivery,' he said, and the catch clicked.

A ribbon of light glowed beneath the door to Rachel's flat. Sticking out of the frame was a metal lock. Beneath, a chunk of wood had been chiselled away. 'Hello?' he called as he pushed open the door.

Books littered the floorboards and shards of glass glinted: the picture frames had been smashed, the modernist prints slashed with a knife, flapping in the breeze billowing in from the open balcony windows.

'Rachel?'

As he passed the sofa, he saw her wallet and car keys still on the table. A glow emanated from the bedroom door. He eased it open.

Rachel lay half naked on the bed. Her arms rested by her hips, two semicircles of red blotting the mattress on either side of her torso. Protruding from between her ribs was a kitchen knife, the blade driven midway down. In the light from the courtyard, the hilt cast the shape of a crucifix on her pale stomach.

Spike rocked on his heels, then forced himself towards the bed. Her eyes were closed save for a crescent of white; automatically his fingers moved to grasp the knife, but he pulled them away when he saw her chest rise and fall.

He took out his phone, noting vacantly that a text had come in: Drew Stanford-Trench. He killed it and tried to think of an ambulance number. Nothing came to mind, so he tried Azzopardi.

'Why aren't you at the flat?' Azzopardi said.

'I need an ambulance.'

'What?'

'A woman's been stabbed at – Christ, where the fuck am I . . .?' He took out his wallet and read the address from Rachel's business card. 'Have you got that?'

'Yes, but –'

Spike spun round, hairs erect on the back of his neck. A sound had come from the sitting room. He slipped the phone in his pocket and crept towards the door.

Cheers carried up from Carnival. Through the net curtains, Spike made out a silhouette moving on the balcony.

A thump from below, followed by a distant yell of pain; Spike clawed the curtains from his face and stepped outside. Hands on railings, he looked down. A man was crouching on the roof of the Skoda. Beyond him on the road lay the oval shape of a painting.

Salib glanced up, then rolled off the car to the pavement below. Spike hoisted a foot onto the balcony railings, ready to jump down after. He stopped: a cry had just come from inside the flat. Salib looked up again and smiled, then limped away down the street, canvas stretcher tucked under one arm. The cry came again, faint and plaintive; Spike re-entered the sitting room in time to hear the rev of a motorbike on the street below.

Rachel's eyes were open. She lay rigid, staring upwards. Spike took hold of her hand. The diameter of the bloodstain behind her had increased. 'Tell them,' she murmured.

Spike squeezed her hand. 'Shh.'

'Tell them I found it.'

'Lie still. I won't leave you.'

'My discovery,' she repeated, eyes burning and insistent.

'I'll tell them,' Spike said. 'I promise.'

Her face relaxed as her hand fell limp in his grasp.

He stayed by her side until the first squall of an ambulance siren overwhelmed the music of Carnival. Then he grabbed her car keys and ran down into the street.

6

Spike hadn't driven a car since failing his test while at law school in London. With the ambulance lights still flashing in his rear-view mirror, he twisted the ignition and steered Rachel's Skoda unsteadily onto the road. He indicated right, and all at once the street began to fall away, dipping into a tunnel and emerging on the road beneath Valletta's city walls. A bus honked aggressively as it drew up behind; realising he was still in first, Spike forced the gearstick into fourth. The Skoda gave a crunch, then started to pick up speed.

His phone was ringing; he fumbled in his pocket, adjusting the wheel to avoid veering off the road into the harbour.

'What the fuck?' Azzopardi said.

'Is Rachel alive?'

'She's with paramedics. They don't know if she'll regain consciousness. She's Maltese, Spike. What the *fuck*?'

'Salib was at the flat when I arrived.'

'Where is he now?'

'On a motorbike. Heading south.'

'Where are *you* now?'

Another blast of a horn; Spike realised he was in second not fourth.

'Where's he going, Spike?'

'I think back to the marina.'

'He'd never go back there. The police are all over it.' There was a pause. 'You're not following him, are you?'

'I'm trying to.'

'Pull out, Spike. You're out of your depth.'

The road disappeared into another tunnel. When it re-emerged, the connection had broken. Spike tossed the phone onto the passenger seat. He was skirting the far side of the St James Ditch, edging towards Floriana. Carnival revellers bustled ahead: he hung a right and continued past a football stadium.

At least the road signs were in English and Maltese. Seeing one for Marsa, he steered towards it. It was then that he remembered Drew Stanford-Trench's text. Eyes flitting from phone screen to windscreen, he pulled up the message. It took a moment to download: *Calypso Lines registered to a Desmond Zammit. 3 yrs ago 1 of its fleet stopped in southern Med for overloading. Carob wood from Libya. No entry on Falcon Freight. Do u have name right?*

Seeing another sign for Marsa, Spike swung into the exit, cutting up a pickup coming the opposite way, a painted fibreglass tiger strapped to its back. A moment later the Skoda was speeding along the road which followed the top of the Marsa sea wall.

7

Spike walked silently past the warehouses, searching for a sign of the motorbike. Nothing but the shadows of ships' masts, twitching on the concrete like giants' fingers.

He found himself outside the safe house. Blue-and-white cordons criss-crossed the gate; two heavy new padlocks closed the hasp. So much for a police presence. Probably all at Carnival with their kids.

He turned back to the marina. Motor launches, skiffs, yachts . . . He stopped by the boat marked *Falcon Freight*. Rust flaked from its broad hull; diesel stains dripped from the fuel cap. Glancing over one shoulder, he moved towards the balustrade and hoisted himself aboard.

The deck was covered in slimy planks; Spike crept along the left-hand gunwale, one hand trailing the railings surrounding it. Peering in at the roofed wheelhouse, he made out an old-fashioned wooden tiller, cracked glass on the dials. Azzopardi had been right on one front – this marina really was a junkyard.

The foredeck was wider and higher than the aft. Sunk into the centre was a wooden compartment, open-topped, about the size of a builders' skip, presumably where the fishermen would empty their catch. A wooden mast rose behind: Spike put a hand to it as he edged around the perimeter of the compartment. A dark shape was propped against the side wall of the wheelhouse. A black, low-slung motorbike.

A sudden sputtering came from the rear of the boat. The decking gave a shiver as a rumble issued from beneath Spike's feet. The engine had been switched on.

Spike's first instinct was to climb the balustrade and leap onto the adjacent vessel. He started calculating distances, then felt the boat lurch forward. Out of sight, mooring ropes were being loosed.

He glanced around, then began climbing down into the sunken compartment. It was two-tiered, with large, deep steps. Once at the base, he found a ledge beneath the lowest step, and rolled beneath it.

The trawler continued slowly out of the marina. Spike saw the reflections of other boats' rigging passing overhead. As they turned towards the open sea, the shadows changed angle on the base of the compartment.

He felt for his phone, drawing it carefully from his pocket. The floorboards he lay on were quivering with vibrations; as he raised the phone to his ear, he saw wood which was lighter in colour, less slimy. Picking up the scent of burning cannabis, he suspended his breathing. A shadow spread over the base of the compartment. A moment later, he caught the twirling sparkle of a butt, and the shadow retreated.

Still lying flat, Spike picked up his phone again and called Azzopardi. The rumble of the engine meant he could talk without detection; it also meant, he realised grimly, that he was unable to hear anything at the other end of the line. Teeth clamped with annoyance, he started to compose a text. A new noise mingled with the engine – rats, scratching at the wood beneath his ear. With painful slowness, he started to type: *On board Falcon Freight, moving out to sea.* Send . . . he waited for the message to go, watching the signal disappear bar by bar as they pulled further away from Malta. He shook the handset, then covered the LED screen with one hand as the shadow appeared again.

The figure began climbing down the steps into the compartment. Legs appeared; Spike recognised Salib's blue canvas trousers. Spike watched him bend down, then lower himself painfully to his knees. In one hand he held a Maglite torch, its powerful yellow beam pooling on the decking. In the other was a screwdriver, which he began twisting into the floorboards.

Once he'd removed two screws, Salib stood and limped to the other side of the compartment. His injured leg was hampering him; as he hoisted a knee onto the first step, Spike rolled from beneath his ledge, raised his body into a crouching position, then got to his feet.

In two silent strides, he was behind Salib. He grabbed his shoulders, hauling him backwards. The torch skittered over the decking, light extinguished, as Salib's head hit the wooden boards with a thud.

Spike charged forward to kick Salib's fist. The screwdriver flew into the air, spinning away onto the upper deck. He planted a second kick on Salib's temple, watching him rotate like a beetle on the slimy decking.

'Where's Zahra?' he shouted down, his voice surprisingly clear against the drone of the engine.

Salib was smiling. Spike moved at him again. This time, as Spike swung his foot, Salib caught the heel, jerking Spike forward so that he landed on his back on the ground beside him.

Spike tried to spring up, but in a moment Salib was straddling him, sinewy thighs clasping the sides of his chest, pinning down his biceps with his knees. The first punch hit Spike's ear, sending a sharp ringing through his skull. The next came from Salib's other fist, connecting with Spike's mouth. Spike tasted blood seeping between his gums, drenching his throat as the third blow hit his cheekbone.

Spike was losing strength. He forced his eyes apart and saw Salib still kneeling above him, raising a fist carefully, before bringing the central knuckle down on the bridge of Spike's nose.

The stinging pierced the fog in Spike's brain; his eyes flooded with salt. He felt Salib adjust position, and in that fraction of a second, the pressure on his biceps reduced enough to allow him to twist his right arm free. As the next blow approached, Spike squeezed his index and middle fingers together into the sign of the cross, then jabbed them up as hard as he could into Salib's throat.

There was a crunch of cartilage as Spike's fingers connected with Salib's Adam's apple. He felt something give as his windpipe collapsed in on itself, one half clamping to the other through some internal suction mechanism of the body.

Spike let his arm fall. Salib was rocking back and forth, eyes bulging, jaw opening and closing like a fish as he fought to suck in air. His hand moved to his throat, fingertips exploring the notch where his Adam's apple had been, like a dent in a Coke can, Spike noted dizzily. Freeing his other arm, he rolled Salib sideways onto the decking.

Spike's nose and chin were sticky with blood. 'Where is she?' he shouted down at Salib's pink and flushed face. 'Where's Zahra?'

Salib's arms and legs were twitching. He blinked upwards, unable to speak, as Spike brought his head in closer, seeing his lips form two distinct words: 'She gone.'

'What?'

'She gone,' Salib mouthed again. Then his lips stretched into a smile and his eyes closed.

Spike collapsed back onto the steps of the compartment. He found he was sobbing, tears diluting the blood. Leaning his head back against the wood, he decided to close his eyes.

8

Spike landed with a judder. Moments later, his body was thrown back into the air, bouncing off a wall before collapsing onto a cold, salty surface. A crunching – part roar, part snapping – filled his ears. He felt himself rise again in the darkness, levitating for an instant before smacking down even harder onto the deck.

He opened his eyes: he was lying beside Salib's corpse, which was slumped face down, nose and mouth submerged in an inch of water. The boat shook again as the roaring grew louder, issuing from below, complemented by a high-pitched whistle. With a sudden panicked violence, Spike thrust out his hands and shoved the body away from him.

Pulling himself up onto the lower step, Spike got to his feet. The boat gave another lurch as he climbed out of the basin, digging his nails into the sodden planks to maintain his grip. Once on the top deck, he stared out in disbelief.

The bow of the boat was wedged against a sheer wall of limestone. To the left and right gaped dark deep caverns. The crunching came from the hull as it butted the cliff face and was rebuffed.

Spike gripped the balustrade as the boat lurched again, propelled by its engine, which was somehow still turning. This time a chunk of limestone fell away and the hull started to swivel lengthways against the cliffs.

Spike braced himself for the next collision, and was thrown sideways as a wall of water sloshed onto the deck; once the floor had steadied, he crawled towards the wheelhouse and pulled himself inside. The motorbike had gone, swept overboard.

A light winked on the fuel gauge; three of the dials had needles jammed to the furthest edge, the others hung inert. Spike twisted the key to off, and the engine stuttered to a halt. He grabbed the tiller, but it was stuck solid as the waves drove the hull against the rocks. A momentary silence, before an acrid stench began to waft across the deck.

Over one shoulder, Spike saw that the stern was now a metre underwater, the bow abnormally raised. Smoke was pouring up from a vent in the rear deck, billowing against the starlit sky.

He felt in his pocket for his phone, but it had been lost in the struggle with Salib. A grey bin bag was wedged beneath the tiller. Opening it up, he found Mifsud's worthless canvas inside, carefully swaddled in an oilskin.

He moved back to the railings, trying to judge the boat's position, ready to throw himself into the water and swim for the cliffs. Beneath his feet, he heard something tapping against the wood. The last throes of the engine? He glanced back at the wheelhouse: the dials were still dead. The tapping came again, deep below the deck. He withdrew from the balustrade, then dropped to one knee and picked up the screwdriver that was rolling on the deck.

On the last step down into the sunken compartment, Spike was thrown forwards as the boat hit the cliffs once more. A hollow popping was coming from above, like gas igniting in a jar. Looking up, he saw darker smoke trailing against the moon.

He lowered his head; in the rosy light, he found Salib's body jammed beneath its ledge. Beside him lay the Maglite. Spike crawled over, grabbed it and clicked the button on the base. A powerful beam of light appeared.

A deeper-throated roar echoed from behind; Spike saw flames licking up from the stern, felt heat on his face. Screwdriver in one hand, torch in the other, he knelt to the half-opened section of decking, fingers stiff with cold and shock. A lighter, plywood board was held down by four screws, two of which had already been removed. Holding the Maglite between his teeth, he started twisting the screwdriver into the remaining threads, drawing out the screws with his shaking wet hands.

Ramming the screwdriver into the edge of the plank, he prised it up and shone the torch down. In the low, cramped compartment, two small faces stared up, black hair soaked with salt water, eyes dazzled by the light.

The younger girl was dark-skinned, almost Zahra but not. Both were sitting on the wet floor, legs in front, one arm tethered awkwardly behind.

'Hold on,' Spike yelled down, before rolling back to Salib's corpse. Running his hands over the body, he wrenched up Salib's T-shirt, pausing for a moment to take in the heraldic emblems set into the arms of his tattoo – falcon, galleon, evil eye – before dipping into his back pocket and pulling out a bunch of keys.

The water was rising below deck, but the girls were unable to stand, restrained by their bindings. Spike lowered himself through the hatch, feeling his feet slither across the solid surface.

The girls' screams increased as the water neared their chests; Spike knelt beside the younger, Maglite in mouth, keys in one hand, feeling below the water with his other.

The cold chains of handcuffs; he plunged his free hand beneath the surface and slid the first key into the lock. It wouldn't turn, so he tried the second. At last he felt the mechanism click, and the younger girl pulled her arm free. She climbed at once to her feet, skidding as she tried desperately to pull herself out through the hatch.

Spike turned to the other girl and delved again beneath the water. He felt again for the lock, then twisted. The girl withdrew her arm, but remained seated, face impassive and staring.

'Zahra,' Spike shouted. 'Is she here?'

'They take her,' the woman said.

'Who?'

'The men.'

'When . . .' Spike began, but a plank of wood in the side of the compartment sprang loose, a plume of black smoke coiling in above the gushing water.

The younger girl was struggling to pull herself onto the upper deck. She was sobbing now; Spike waded through the water and lifted her bodily up through the gap. The older woman had still not moved, so Spike reached again beneath the water and clawed at her hips, coughing as the fumes began to fill the compartment. She was too weak to climb, but he dragged her towards the hatch, then felt the pressure on his arms reduce as the younger girl started pulling her up from the other side.

The Maglite glinted beneath the water; Spike retrieved it and shone it around the cabin, refusing to believe that Zahra was gone.

A shout from above; the water was cascading in now, chillier, as though issuing from a deeper recess of the sea. Spike lifted his arms through the hatch and hauled himself out, slumping onto the base of the compartment, then stumbling up the steps to the top deck, catching his foot on Salib's stiffening corpse as he climbed up towards the cold air. He found the women huddled together in front of the wheelhouse, arms looped around each other.

The boat started to list, weighed down by its flooded hold. There was a fizzing as fire met seawater, followed by a bubbling, swarming sound like bees. The younger girl grabbed the balustrade; she stared at Spike with bloodshot eyes as she disappeared, sliding beneath the railings feet first. The bow rose up, rolling Spike backwards. He grabbed the railings and watched the older woman follow her friend overboard, her shriek silenced as she hit the water.

A brighter, more intense red burned in the heart of the fire. Spike wondered if this signalled an impending explosion, until he made out the sound of a siren, and recognised the flashing light of a police launch.

He worked his way along the balustrade. Now that the engine had died, the boat had drifted back from the cliffs, revealing the shape of an island beyond, Comino perhaps, with the dark triangular rocks of the Blue Lagoon protruding like teeth from the water. He glanced back, then slid his legs beneath the railings, swinging from the bars and feeling himself fall gracefully through the air until the cool water embraced him.

✳

She waits. The boat has become a van, the sea a winding road. But he will look for her. She knows he will keep looking, and in this she finds comfort.

Chapter Eleven

I

Spike sat at a table for one on the restaurant terrace. A family of British tourists were standing on the harbourside, the father snapping photographs of the *luzzi*, the child's face hidden by a mask in the shape of a falcon.

Another *bajtra* ordered, Spike returned to the *Sunday Times of Malta*. An entire six-page spread was dedicated to the man known as '*is-Salib*', 'the Cross', and his orgy of violence. Initial articles focused on the continuing mystery of his identity: the Prime Minister of Malta insisted there was no record of him coming from any part of the archipelago; Italy, and Sicily in particular, also denied him citizenship. The current hypothesis was that he hailed from the Balkan peninsula, apparently because his unregistered vessel, *Falcon Freight*, bore certain similarities to ships constructed in the eastern Adriatic. His motorbike, now dredged from the sea, had been reported stolen from an address in St Julian's ten weeks earlier. A cautionary tale, one commentator said, highlighting the flaws of the Schengen Area, which allowed criminals free movement through Europe.

No mention was made of Salib's connection to John Petrovic, nor of the number of times his boat had been seen moored in the Marsa docks. His most recent victims had all awoken in hospital to find themselves fast-tracked for EU passports, their desire to speak about their ordeal fading soon after.

Spike turned the page. Salib, it was believed, had circulated among the vulnerable migrant community of Malta, offering women the chance of hotel work in Sicily. After luring them to an abandoned warehouse, he had drugged and raped them, awaiting the cover of Carnival to move them to his boat. One girl, Dinah, had managed to escape the warehouse, but been killed in the attempt. Guessing that the police would now be close behind, Salib had scaled down his operation and selected just a few victims to take to his boat, where he had concealed them for three days in appalling conditions.

Salib was also implicated in the deaths of a parish priest, Father Philip de Maro, and of a middle-aged couple, David and Teresa Mifsud. The stabbing of an art historian, Rachel Cassar, had resulted in the victim being airlifted to a specialist unit in Palermo, where her condition was said to be stable. While the police were still trying to connect these seemingly unrelated crimes, it was believed that Salib had been pursuing a painting by the Maltese artist, Lorenzo da Gozo, *The Martyrdom of St Agatha*, which was thought to have perished in the sinking of his ship off Comino. Unbeknown to him, the painting was only considered to have been worth a few hundred euros.

Set into the text below was a headshot of Spike, the 'Gibraltar lawyer' who had helped the police locate Salib's boat and had single-handedly saved the lives of two of his victims. Alongside was a large colour photograph of Zahra, the inclusion of which had been a condition of Spike's agreement to speak to the press. '*Seen Zahra?*' asked the caption. '*Then call this number. Substantial reward.*'

Elsewhere, ordinary Maltese news was already creeping back in. '*This year's Carnival "best ever", claims President*'; '*Calls for referendum on divorce reform*'; '*Five stars for Paceville Hilton*' . . .

Spike raised his glass but found it empty. The restaurant owner approached. 'Another?'

'Just the bill, please.'

'It's on the house, Mr Sanguinetti.'

Spike walked back to the harbourfront. On the jetty, a group of fishermen were cleaning their nets. One looked over, eyes narrowed between mutton-chop sideburns. Spike looked back, then continued past.

2

As Spike arrived at the flat, he saw a curtain twitching in the balcony of Palazzo Malaspina: the Baron and Baroness, watching as usual, worrying. His reflection in the hallway mirror showed the Steri-Strips still bisecting the bridge of his nose – according to the doctors, it would always be a little crooked. With his thickening beard he was starting to look a lot like Uncle David. He turned away into the kitchen.

Drying on the table were the contents of his pockets – wallet, credit cards, passport. His phone had been lost at sea, one advantage of which was an end to any more angry or concerned calls from Gibraltar – Jessica, Galliano, Stanford-Trench. The only person he'd spoken to on his new Maltese mobile was his father, who'd seemed entirely unconcerned by his son's failure to return home. Spike checked it now for messages, hoping for some news from Azzopardi, a response to the article in *The Times*. Nothing.

He picked up Salib's Maglite, which had somehow clung on in his pocket, and went into the sitting room. Since the electricity had been cut in the flat, its powerful beam was proving essential.

The cellar had been another welcome discovery, revealed when the rug covering its hatch had been taken away for auction. Spike fingered up its metal hoop and descended the narrow staircase.

Flashing the torch around the wine racks, he chose two bottles of a surprisingly good Maltese red, then steered himself back up.

Yesterday's empties he filled with candles, lighting them off the gas hob, the one utility which still worked.

As he sat down at the table, his thoughts moved again to Zahra, imagining scenarios in which she could be safe. Stuck in one of the camps after losing her passport. Or back home in Morocco, having left the country the day of their argument. He tried to picture her in Tangiers, in a foulard and kaftan, reunited with her cousins, but then the horrors began to return – Dinah lying on the pathologist's slab, her baby's icy eyes . . . He poured himself more wine, but the images worsened until Zahra herself reappeared, held down beneath Salib, or drugged in a massage parlour as a laughing Italian tore at her dress. He remembered Salib's last words: 'She gone.' Gone where? he asked himself as he opened another bottle. Dead or alive, her body, her bones, her face, her heart – they had to be *somewhere*, and the sickening certainty of this made him keep drinking until sleep came stumbling in.

3

An unknown ringtone wheedled its way into Spike's brain; he ignored it, then realised it belonged to his new phone. Rolling from between the sheets, he loped through the flat into the kitchen. A Gibraltarian number. He killed the call and went back to bed.

His hangover vied with the pain across the bridge of his nose. Dawn was leaking in through the boarded-up bedroom window. The phone went off again, a message presumably. He waited for it to stop. When it went off a fourth time, he moved reluctantly back to the kitchen. '*What?*'

'Thank God!'

'Jessica?'

'Why the fuck don't you answer your phone, Spike? I've been trying to reach you for three days.'

'How did you get this number?'

'I found it in your father's bedroom. While I was packing him a bag.'

Spike stared at the empty wine bottles, their necks seamy with melted wax.

'Your dad's in hospital, Spike.'

He pulled up a chair and sat. 'Heart?'

'Lungs.'

Spike let out a low groan.

'He's in ICU. Apparently they got it early. Something to do with his syndrome, pneumo . . .'

'Pneumothorax.'

'He kept asking for you.'

'I'm on the next plane.' Spike got to his feet. 'Thank you, Jess.'

'Any time.'

He hung up, then moved to the sink. The water came out in a dribble. He waited for enough to collect in his palm, then smeared it on his face, tasting limescale, sweat, stale wine. His stomach heaved and he threw up into the sink. There was insufficient tap water to wash away the vomit.

4

Spike walked alone down Triq ir-Repubblicca, airline ticket in hand. The next flight home was at 9 p.m. He checked the time now: midday.

Two bicycles leaned against the facade of the Baron's palazzo. He tried the knocker, and the door opened to reveal a squat dark youth in a tight Lycra T-shirt.

'Is the Baron in?'

'*Che dici?*'

'I wanted to say goodbye.'

The youth puffed out his chest, a buff Italian homunculus.

'Michael?' Spike enunciated. 'Or Natalya?'

The youth signalled with his bullet head for Spike to enter. Music boomed from the first floor, duetting with the whine of a vacuum cleaner. The youth called to the top of the stairs, then gestured for Spike to go up.

The shutters on the balcony were closed, the silver nef glinting on its console table as though newly polished. Clara was hoovering next door, a CD player on the dining-room table pumping out a pan-pipe version of 'Total Eclipse of the Heart'.

'I'm looking for Michael,' Spike shouted.

Clara clicked off the Hoover with a prod of the foot. 'You wanna Baron?'

'Or Baroness –' Spike broke off as his eye was caught by the portrait above the dining-room table.

'Inna the countryside,' Clara said. 'Wardija. Hunting lodge . . .'

Spike switched off the stereo, still staring up at the Baron's monastic robes. Set into the white arms of his Maltese cross was a now familiar sequence of emblems – falcon, galleon, evil eye . . .

Clara's head appeared between him and the painting. 'You need doctor again?' she said, pointing to his nose.

Spike put a hand to his face: his nose was bleeding. Clara held out a tissue but he wiped his bristly upper lip with the back of his hand.

'Take message?' she said.

'What? No . . . I'll go myself. Wardija, you say?'

'Wardija.'

5

The taxi wound slowly up the hill. The sun seemed higher in the sky, and for the first time Spike could sense the true intensity of the climate, a drier, crueller heat than Gibraltar. He turned away from the window, thinking again of the Baron's cloak in the portrait. He was certain he'd seen the same heraldic devices in Salib's tattoo.

The driver braked. 'See that?' he said, pointing up through the windscreen.

Spike leaned forward. A small, plaster-of-Paris madonna swung like a censer from the rear-view mirror. 'What?' he asked impatiently.

The driver opened his door and got out. Suppressing his annoyance, Spike did the same. A low, drystone wall ran along the near side of the road. Cacti and shrubs grew beyond; Spike heard the first cicadas of the season chirruping in the undergrowth.

'I'm in a bit of a hurry . . .'

'Up there,' the driver said, pointing into the bright blue sky.

Spike formed a visor with his hand: a black dot hung in the air three hundred feet above.

'Maltese falcon,' the driver said.

'You must have good eyesight.'

The falcon hovered, wingtips fluttering.

'It's a subspecies of peregrine,' the driver went on. 'Very rare.' He put an arm across Spike's chest as he turned back towards the car. 'Patience . . .'

The falcon had dipped down a few feet. 'They can see everything from up there,' the driver said. 'Nothing gets past them. Here we go . . .' He nodded at the field on the far side of the wall. At its edge, grazing on some goat-cropped grass, sat a baby rabbit. Spike looked back up at the falcon, which had dropped down a few more metres, hanging in front of the sun.

'Any second . . .'

All of a sudden, the falcon tucked its wings behind its back and arrowed downwards. Its line was straight, gathering speed as it neared the ground. The rabbit gambolled a few paces towards greener pastures, but the falcon was locked on like a missile, wheeling around at the last moment, then smacking into the rabbit claws first with a thump that was audible even from this side of the field. Clamped together, bird and beast rolled away until concealed by a cactus.

'. . . now,' the driver concluded with a smile as he got back into the cab. A thin scream cut the air. 'Wardija, was it?' he said.

6

The village spread over the brow of the hill, a vista of the sea and St Paul's Islands in one direction, sloped terraced fields in the other. Stone walls flanked the road, delineating the grounds of the knights' various hunting lodges. 'It's the Malaspina place, right?' the driver said.

'Yes.'

'You a friend of the Baron's?'

'He knew my uncle.'

'He's a good man. They were going to close down my daughter's school in Mdina. He brought in outside investment, now we have the best school in the area.'

As they drove past a set of wrought-iron gates, Spike glanced in at an alley of gnarled olive trees stretching into the distance. A crenellated stone wall ran off the gate, the bell tower of a private chapel rising behind. The wall adjoined what looked like a miniature castle. It was built with the same golden limestone as the houses of Valletta, though the statues in the decorative niches were crumbling and smashed.

'Here we are,' the driver said, stopping outside a smaller door in the wall.

'Can you wait for me here?' Spike asked.

The driver adjusted his meter, then picked up a hardback from the passenger seat.

Spike got out. The door led to some kind of gatehouse: the main entrance to the castle seemed too fortified to be in regular use. It had a vertical letter box in the centre and a rusty bell in the jamb alongside. Nailed into the wood was a dented metal sign warning 'Beware of the Dog'.

Spike held down the stiff button and heard a distant chime above the saw of the cicadas. He waited for a few minutes, then returned to the cab. 'Have you got a pen and paper?'

The driver passed him a pad. Back at the wooden door, Spike wrote a brief note: 'The painting wasn't lost at sea. Meet me at the flat at 6 p.m. Spike.' He folded the paper in two, scribbled 'Michael' on the front and pushed it through the letter box. Worth a punt, he thought to himself as the cab drove back to Valletta.

7

A van was parked opposite the Mifsud flat, hazard lights on. 'You still here?' the furniture remover asked as Spike unlocked the front door.

Within five minutes all the remaining crates had been piled into the remover's van. 'Sign and date,' the remover said, handing over a clipboard.

'How about this one?' Spike asked, pointing at the hallway mirror. 'It's got a sticker on it.'

'You won't get that off without bringing half the wall down with it,' the remover said. 'Take it up with the landlord.'

The door slammed. The light was fading, so Spike fired up some candles, then went into the bedroom and set about packing. His wallet and passport were finally dry; he pocketed them, then moved to the bathroom, seeing a solitary stool unflushed in the lavatory, leaking colour like a tea bag.

Shaking his head in revulsion, he swept his wash things into the sponge bag, knocking over a shaving mirror, which broke in two on the bathroom floor. As he gathered the pieces, he caught sight of his reflection. He stared down, motionless. 'Surely not,' he said aloud, then turned back towards the hallway.

Standing in front of the mirror, he examined not his own image but the dimensions of its oval frame. Six shiny brackets were fixed to the rim, screwed directly into the wall. He brushed one with his thumb and found a fine plaster dust on the skin.

He reached for the frame and pulled it towards him. It held rigid. Crouching down, he saw a gap between the mirror and the wall. The tools in the flat had been removed, but he found a knife sharpener in the kitchen, its metal prong solid and stiff. Pacing back to the hallway, he shoved the implement down the back of the mirror and started prising it away. A crackling came from the wood, so he stopped, then banged the handle with the heel of his hand so it sank in deeper. This time when he prised it away, the bracket started to bend, flakes of plaster trickling down onto the skirting board.

He repeated the process for each screw, then threw the knife sharpener aside and began pulling with his hands. A moment later, he stumbled backwards as the mirror came free, landing with a heavy crack on the hallway floor.

Spike bent down, picking up the outer edge of the frame and rolling it over. The mirror tinkled and clattered to a rest beside the door. His hand went to his mouth and he tasted blood; a new cut, this time to his ring finger.

The mirror backing was fixed down by four large metal clasps. Spike slid them one by one across the frame, his fingertip bloody.

As he lifted away the backing, he saw a wrinkled, reddish-brown canvas beneath. He wiped his hands on his trousers, then pincered up one of the frayed edges with thumb and forefinger. Heart thumping, he flipped it over, then took a step backwards.

Staring up at him was *The Martyrdom of St Agatha*. His eyes began to circle the oval canvas. A tickling fluttered in his stomach. Written in black at the base, along the lighter band once hidden by the frame, was the signature, 'F. Michelangelo'.

8

Spike triple-locked the front door, then slid the bolts in place. After checking the security clasps on each window, he tested the plywood in the bedroom. Satisfied, he cut a strip from an almost-clean T-shirt and wound it around his bleeding hand. Only then did he touch the canvas again, carrying it by one corner into the kitchen, where he laid it down on the table.

He drank a measure of rum, then sat. The candles flickered in their bottles. Arching his neck over the table, he stared down. The painting had evidently been cleaned, as his eyes took in details he had missed in the photographs. A single tab of tooth between Agatha's lips. A metal piercing in the left lobe of the jailer's cauli-flowered ear. A spray of ruby droplets as the jaws of the clippers bit into Agatha's remaining breast.

The horror of the painting was different to the *Beheading of St John*, Spike thought. Caravaggio's *St John* had been static – theat-rical, Rachel had called it. In this painting, Saint Agatha's fingers weren't frozen in time, they were twisting in a continuing agony. The amputation of her breasts seemed more than just a depiction of pagan cruelty: it felt like the death of motherhood, of morality, of optimism. The man who'd painted this hadn't been buoyed up by his newly attained knighthood: he'd lost all hope, betrayed by his nature, signing his name for the last time as 'Brother Michelangelo', aware that his imminent expulsion from the order would reveal him for what he was: a violent criminal on the run.

Spike looked up at the darkened curtains. He'd lost track of time – it was 6.30 p.m., just two and a half hours until his plane left. As he got to his feet, he sensed something move at the periphery of his vision. Turning his head, he saw a man standing in the kitchen doorway. Clamped to his shoulder was a rifle.

The man wore a checked hunter's shirt. His neat moustache twitched in amusement.

'Good evening, Spike,' said the Baron.

9

'You're early,' Spike said, sitting back down.

The Baron was pointing the rifle at Spike's chest. 'I wanted to surprise you.'

'How did you get in? Through the bedroom window?'

The Baron moved forward, rifle still pressed to shoulder. 'Didn't you know? There's a tunnel that links the flat's cellar to the palazzo.' He chuckled. 'Funny, I thought Natalya had told you.'

Spike remembered what Zahra had said on the ferry – stories of escape routes built to protect Valletta's wealthy against Ottoman pirates. 'Is that how Salib got in?' he asked. 'On the night he murdered my uncle and aunt?'

The Baron's eyes flicked towards the table, where the canvas still lay, surrounded by guttering candles. 'You found it then,' he said.

Spike nodded.

'Not lost at sea.'

'No.'

'Where was David hiding it?'

'Behind the mirror.'

The Baron smiled. 'Your uncle always enjoyed the sight of his own reflection.' He lowered his arms slightly. The rifle was now pointing at Spike's thigh.

'He confided in you, didn't he?' Spike said, edging his chair back. 'Told you about his great discovery. And how did you reward him? By paying some thug to steal the painting.'

The Baron shook his head, gaze moving again towards the table.

'Did you pay Salib to murder them too? To rape my aunt, then kill them both? Or did he use his own initiative?'

'You seem to hold your uncle in very high regard.'

'He was a good man.'

The Baron's eyes shone in delight. 'Well, you're right about one thing. David did tell me about the painting. He was bragging about a letter he'd found in the Notarial Archives. From a knight of the order to his valet. Written in 1798, just days before the arrival of Napoleon. The knight didn't want to risk losing his property to the French, so he ordered his valet to misattribute the Caravaggio. The valet changed the inventory, the knight died, and the painting was lost. Do you know why he told me?'

'You were his friend.'

'Greed, Spike. He was going to try and sell it, and he thought I'd have the connections to help him find a buyer.'

'You can't sell a stolen Caravaggio.'

'Not on the open market. David might only have got a fraction of the value, but it would have been more than enough for him and Teresa to retire on. There are plenty of people who'd like to own one, even if only they could enjoy it.'

'My uncle wasn't interested in money.'

There was pity in the Baron's tone now. 'You don't understand human nature at all, do you? Everyone's interested in money

– even David. He was so scared about leaving the painting in the chapel, so afraid someone else might find it, that I suggested he bring it home.'

Spike edged his chair back another inch. 'Then all you had to do was pick a night when they were out – and you had an alibi – and send in Salib to steal the painting.'

Spike checked the Baron's face; his moustache quivered, as though he were trying not to succumb to some wickedly amusing anecdote.

'Except they came home early,' Spike said. 'Surprised Salib.'

The Baron took another step closer.

'You used me,' Spike went on. 'You learned from my father about David's plan to return to Gozo, so you sent Salib there to check if he'd put the painting back in the chapel. But it wasn't there. When Salib attacked me in Marsa, you only called him off because you thought I might finally be closing in on it. Otherwise, you'd have let me burn.'

The Baron seemed to have lost interest.

'Then when you saw Rachel Cassar carrying an oval-shaped canvas from the flat, you contacted Salib and told him to steal it. What did you think would happen? That he'd ask her politely?'

He turned his head back to Spike, irritated now. 'A man cannot steal what belongs to him. That painting was commissioned by the Order of St John. It was produced in secret by Caravaggio while he was still in prison, in exchange for his safe passage to Italy after his expulsion from the order. One last masterpiece before they lost him for ever. That was why so few people saw it, even before it disappeared. Such a bargain would have caused a scandal. So it was kept for the order's private delectation. A reminder that even in brutality, in dissolution, God's beauty can exist. And within beauty, lies hope.'

Spike sensed that the Baron had rehearsed this speech. 'Why not just tell David to surrender the painting to the authorities?

Let it hang with the other Caravaggios in the oratory? You could have enjoyed it there.'

'In that circus?' the Baron spat. 'No, *The Martyrdom* was painted for the order. It belongs to us.' He raised the rifle back to his shoulder. 'Now stand up.'

Spike got to his feet.

'Into the bedroom.'

Spike stepped backwards, hands in the air; as he passed the table, the Baron stopped before the Caravaggio, lost in its terrible beauty. Creeping forward, Spike looped his arms around the Baron's flanks, pinning the rifle in front. A bullet fired up into the ceiling, cratering the plaster. There was a delay as both Spike and the Baron watched the dust particles land on the canvas. No sound from upstairs: Clara and her friend were long gone. Then the Baron began to struggle.

10

Spike wrestled the Baron to the floor. Grabbing the barrel of the rifle, he prised it from his fingers. It came away easily, and he threw it aside, then rolled the Baron onto his back.

'What was his name?'

Another shower of dust dropped from the ceiling, creating an iron-filings flare as it burned in the flame of a candle. The Baron tried to get to his feet, desperate to protect the painting, but Spike pressed down on his shoulders, pinning him to the floor. 'I asked you a question, Michael. Who was Salib?'

'Nobody . . . nothing.' The Baron's voice was urgent and high; smoke from the burning plaster dust was now rising from the table. 'Just someone I used to get things done –'

'Did you pay him?'

'In a sense; I knew he had interests in Sicily.'

'So you gave him John Petrovic. Someone he could use to source vulnerable women and children.'

The Baron bared his teeth. 'The immigrant camps are a blight on Malta. A second Great Siege. Why do you think the police have turned a blind eye all these years? They breed like rabbits . . .'

'So you made them into a commodity. Allowed dozens of women to be sold into prostitution.'

'What happens in Italy is not my concern.'

'And the tattoo?'

The Baron's expression softened. He gave a gentle, almost paternal smile. 'Salib may have been damaged, but he was a patriot. He came to see me as something of a father figure.'

'The son you never had.'

'Perhaps.'

'He was a rapist. A murderer –'

'So was Caravaggio,' the Baron called out, glancing back at the painting. He started to stand but Spike shoved him forward against the table. A bottle fell, leaking rum as it rolled, knocking over one of the candlesticks. An orange glow rose from the table, followed by the sweet aroma of burning alcohol.

'My painting,' the Baron gasped.

Spike wrapped an arm around his throat. 'Where's Zahra?'

'Who?'

'Who did Salib sell her to?'

On the table, the flames were being drawn towards the hole in the ceiling, greedily licking at the exposed wood.

'Tell me!'

The Baron strained like a dog at the lead. 'I don't know. I swear!'

The panic in the Baron's voice was persuasive. As soon as Spike relaxed his grip, he leapt forward to the table, shielding his face from the glare. The heat was unbearable, flames spreading along the ceiling, so Spike retreated to the hallway. He realised he'd locked the front door from the inside; the keys were in his suitcase. Smoke blocked the route to the bedroom. Doubling back, he stopped outside the kitchen door, seeing the Baron still inside, one arm stretching towards the canvas, which lay just out of reach on the table, glowing as its ancient softening paint reflected the flames.

'Michael!'

The Baron swivelled his head. His faded blond hair dripped over his brow. Sweat streaked his face. He grinned, then looked away.

Smoke was filling the room; Spike could no longer see into the kitchen. He found the Maglite on the desk then moved to the cellar hatchway.

As he descended, the air began to cool. On reaching the bottom, he heard a thin, sharp scream amid the roar and crackle of the flames, like air escaping a burning log, or a rabbit pinioned by a falcon.

He clicked on the torch and moved more deeply into the cellar.

11

Squinting in the glare of the Maglite, Spike saw that one of the wine racks had been pulled away from the wall. He dragged it towards him and found a mouldy sheet of plywood behind. He pushed the plywood aside. The mouth of a tunnel gaped.

He glanced back. Above, the hatchway door was open, a reddish glow emanating from a furling cover of smoke. Flames crackled; he turned back to the tunnel, crouched down and stepped inside.

The walls and roof of the tunnel were made of carved blocks of limestone. The ground was damp; he flashed the torch downwards and saw the Baron's dainty footprints still in the muddy clay.

He pressed on, head low, eyes staring ahead. He ought to have been beneath the main part of the Baron's palazzo by now; at any point, the tunnel would open up and he would find himself inside the roomy, vaulted cellars.

The tunnel curved to the right; as he rounded the corner, he stopped. Two small, solid metal gateways stood side by side. Both were rusty brown, the central bolts unfastened.

Spike looked again for footprints but saw none on the dry rock floor. He tried to picture the layout of the palazzo, then chose the left-hand gate, seeing his arm stretch towards it, illuminated by the shaking beam of the Maglite.

The hinge was stiff; he pushed one side and the hatch swung open. The sudden breeze on his face reassured him and he edged inside crabwise.

The tunnel grew broader on the other side: tree roots had inveigled their way through the blocks of limestone, dangling down like jungle creepers. Spike brushed them from his face, relieved to find the tunnel curving again to the left, directing him beneath what he calculated must be the downstairs kitchen of the palazzo.

He stopped. A brick wall blocked the way. He raised the torch and saw it was no more than three feet high, leaving room to clamber over.

The wall was curved, one half of a circle. The circle continued on the other side, a round dark space in between.

Spike peered over the edge and pointed his torch downwards. From below came a faint, penny-sized gleam. He shone the beam around the walls of the shaft. A well had been sunk into the tunnel, blocking the way forward.

Spike aimed the torch upwards, seeing a rusty chain dangling, perhaps once having held a bucket. The blackness above suggested the wellhead had been sealed off.

Cursing, he turned and started to retrace his steps. As he rounded the corner, he stopped again. A dark fog filled the tunnel. His eyes began to water. Smoke was streaming towards him: opening the metal hatchway had created a vacuum.

He lumbered back towards the well, the smoke just a few yards behind. He waited to see if it would be drawn up into the shaft, but it swept on over the circular wall and into the tunnel beyond.

Spike's sinuses burned with the fumes; he tried to breathe in, but his lungs refused. Coughing, he shone the torch over the top of the well, checking distances. Already the smoke was too thick for the beam to penetrate. The only object illuminated was the hanging, bucketless chain; Spike reached up and grabbed it, feeling his hand slide down rings coated in centuries of greasy muck.

A newly discovered claustrophobia started to tighten his chest. He flung the Maglite ahead into the darkness, then took hold of the chain with both hands. A moment later, his body was swinging in a slow arc above the well. The wall on the other side must have been slightly higher, as he felt himself slam against it, knees knocking into the curved sides of the shaft. Silence, then a distant plip as some loosened chunks of masonry hit the water. What a way to go, Spike thought as he held on. An hour treading water in a disused well before slipping unseen into the mire.

Breath held, he released the chain with one hand, then grasped at the rim of the wall with the other. His left arm strained under his weight; another set of splashes followed as his feet dislodged more stone. Arms trembling, he released the chain with his left hand, catching the top of the wall just in time. With the last of his strength he hauled himself up, then collapsed onto the damp tunnel floor on the other side.

12

It was tempting to rest, but smoke was still pouring into the tunnel. Beside him lay the torch, its beam shining boldly into the darkness, pointing the way. He struggled back to his feet and pressed onwards.

Once through the main cloud of smoke, he stopped to get a sense of his bearings, breathing in deeply as he shone the torch around. He found that the walls were no longer made of carved blocks: the passageway had been bored directly into the limestone, its surface pitted and pale like Stilton. He felt for his phone, then searched in vain for a signal. In his pocket were his wallet and passport; at least when his bones were found, he'd be easy to identify.

The smoke was catching him up, so he resumed his slow journey forward, clipping his head against the greasy roof as the tunnel narrowed. An opening appeared to the right: in the torchlight he saw another tunnel branching off. He was deep within it before he realised the end was bricked up. Groaning as he reversed like a horse in a stable, he continued along the main artery.

The torch flickered, damaged from its flight over the well. Spike's head was dizzy in the putrid air; he knocked the side of the torch on his palm, almost sobbing before it sputtered back to life. He felt his breathing steady as the darkness receded. He needed to focus his mind, to find a way out. If not, who would look for Zahra?

The tunnel ended in a small dank puddle beneath a shelf of limestone. He tried to turn, but the way was too tight. Feeling his lungs sting, he realised the smoke had found him even here, the cloud just a few yards behind, edging closer. He would die down here like a mole in its burrow.

He shut his eyes and waited for the stench to overwhelm him. Surprised to find himself still breathing, he opened them again and saw the smoke rising in front of him like a will-o'-the-wisp. He followed its path up with the torch beam and saw a round metal shape above his head.

Finding the air for one last breath, he stepped beneath the manhole cover and shoved upwards with his palms. The left-hand edge moved, so he focused his energy on that side, legs apart like a weightlifter, driving upwards. A sliver of light shone in; he shoved harder, twisting his arms until the cover slid to one side, rattling like a giant coin before coming to a standstill.

He pushed his head up through the gap, smoke billowing from around his neck. Shaking off a halo of dust, he made out the aisle of a church. Wooden chairs were spread on either side, an altar in front, Jesus waving down from the frescoed ceiling flanked by a company of angels.

Light-headed, he started to haul himself out. Smoke was still seeping up through the open grate as he pushed the cover back in place, seeing its ancient iron carved with an eight-pointed cross, the symbol of the Knights of Malta.

Spike made his way up the aisle. The back door of the church was unlocked; he pushed it open and emerged into a dark residential street.

A noise came from the distance: the slow lazy wail of a siren. A red light flickered in the sky, so high and fierce that it suggested the fire had spread from the Mifsud flat and that the whole of the Baron's palazzo must now be ablaze.

He breathed in the night air, then turned back to the church. Set above the lintel was a bas-relief of the madonna. Her eyes were pointing south. The direction of the airport, Spike thought, tapping his pocket for his passport.

He set off through Valletta. The sirens grew louder. This time, he didn't look back.

PART THREE

Gibraltar

Chapter Twelve

I

Spike sat at his desk, staring through the French windows. The date palm which grew from the patio of Galliano & Sanguinetti rustled in the breeze. The direction of its fronds suggested that the poniente wind had switched to a levanter. Spring was beginning in Gibraltar, fairer weather on the way.

He returned to the loan agreement and managed to mark up another page before his mind drifted again. Moving back to his laptop, he opened Zahra's website. He'd just paid Google to include it on the first page of hits under 'Missing Persons' and sure enough it came up at once, her photograph in the centre, the reward detailed with a link to his Hotmail. He checked the account. Nothing but spam.

'Working hard?'

Peter Galliano was leaning nonchalantly on the doorpost. His cream linen suit hung a little more loosely on his shoulders: three weeks filling in for Spike at the magistrates' court had shaved off some weight. His expression changed as he saw the website open on Spike's laptop. '*Gruño?*' he enquired gently.

Spike shook his head.

Galliano stroked his goatee, then brightened as he held out a computer printout. 'Got some potential new business,' he said. 'Application for a shipwreck salvage.' He placed the piece of paper on the edge of Spike's desk like bait. 'Is the vessel in Gibraltarian waters or Spanish?' he asked, backing towards the door. 'Who can possibly say . . .?'

Rufus Sanguinetti frowned through his bifocals at last week's *Sunday Times of Malta*. 'I always told you David was innocent,' he said, laying the paper on his knees. 'And they still haven't put a name to the brute who did it?'

'He's one of those people who just slips beneath the radar.'

'Not in Gib he wouldn't.'

Spike looked around the hospital ward. By the opposite bed, a small boy in a yarmulke sat reading to his grandfather. Next to him, an old woman in a headscarf worked her prayer beads as a wrinkled Moroccan stared up at the ceiling. It was like an advert for racially harmonious health care.

'What does the Baron make of it all?' Rufus said.

Seeing the oxygen tubing still looped beneath his father's nose, Spike decided to save that part of the story for later. 'He's pretty incensed.'

'I'm not in the least surprised.'

A doctor was crossing the ward towards them.

'There's Doc Caruana,' Rufus hissed. 'A good Maltese surname if ever there was one.'

'I'd better get on, Dad.'

'Righto. You do what you have to do.'

Spike squeezed his father's dry bony hand, then joined Dr Caruana at the edge of the ward.

'I think we can release your father in a day or two,' the doctor said.

'Keep him for longer if you like.'

Dr Caruana smiled. 'He'll need to change his lifestyle, of course. Less stress. No more foreign travel. It's critical we reduce the pressure on his cardiopulmonary tissue. I believe you're the primary carer, so I'd understand if –'

'It's fine. Thank you.'

Spike could feel the doctor's keen eyes scanning his frame. 'You do realise Marfan syndrome is hereditary. Have you thought about getting checked out? Wouldn't take more than an afternoon?'

Spike shook his head. 'See you tomorrow, Doctor.'

3

The glass-and-steel tower blocks of the Europort held offices for online gambling firms, empty headquarters for shelf companies, sets of modern apartments. To the constant anger of the Spanish, the land they were built on was reclaimed from the sea. Only twenty years ago, Spike would have been up to his neck in salt water.

He stopped by an estate agency in the ground floor of one of the blocks. A property was being advertised in the window, a white-painted Genoese house on the eastern side of the Rock: wrought-iron balcony, sea view. First-floor sitting room lined with bookshelves ... Feeling his chest constrict a little, Spike continued towards Line Wall Road.

The Rock loomed ahead, banner cloud gathering around its peak like smoke from a semi-dormant volcano. Herring gulls circled the crags, preparing to nest. Ahead on Queensway, a lollipop lady held up traffic, helping a group of children to cross. Spike let them pass, then entered the Old Town, seeing a Union Jack draped from a window, a Gibraltarian flag alongside, the levanter breeze fluttering both in harmony.

He nodded at a second cousin, then turned into Irish Town, where an outpost of the Royal Gibraltar Police Force nestled reassuringly beside two long-established pubs.

4

Spike sat with Jessica outside the Clipper pub, sipping a mug of Earl Grey tea. Beneath the table lay General Ironside, muzzle resting on Jessica's feet.

'So you're clear about tomorrow?' Jessica said.

'Two o'clock in Hamish's room.'

'Suite.'

'In Hamish's suite at the Rock Hotel. Then I head downstairs at two thirty with the other groomsmen to meet the guests. Service starts at three.'

'Buttonhole?'

'Sorry. First, I pick up my buttonhole from the florist.'

'Not that it'll make much difference. Your face still looks terrible.' Jessica reached over and put a hand on his. 'Any news on Zahra?'

Spike withdrew his hand and shook his head.

'What's your plan?'

'Keep checking in with Interpol and Europol. Wait till my dad gets out of hospital, then carry on looking.'

Jessica drank her tea.

'So are you out on the town tonight?' Spike said, hearing the forced jollity in his voice. 'Last day of freedom?'

'Think I'll leave that to Hamish.'

'Oh?'

'It's his stag do. They're spending the afternoon checking out the apes on the Rock, then it's James Bond night at the casino. They've been watching the Gibraltar scenes from *The Living Daylights* in his hotel room.'

'Suite.'

Jessica smiled. 'I'm spending the night at home. My brother's over from Madrid. Mum's cooking us *calentita*. Come by if you're at a loose end.'

'I promised to meet Drew.'

Jessica raised an eyebrow.

'Don't worry; I'll be on form for tomorrow.'

She fixed her police hat on her head, then stood. General Ironside followed, stumpy tail wagging. As soon as she passed Spike the lead, his tail fell.

'He has good taste.'

Jessica blushed. 'I'll miss him.'

Spike crouched down to the General, holding a hand beneath his muzzle. His nose twitched as he drew in Rufus's scent. His tail began to wag once more, and they set off together towards Main Street.

5

Sitting at an indoor table of the All's Well, Spike thought about the last time he'd been there – Piers Harrington, hunched at a corner table, speaking Serbian. The interior of the pub was busier tonight, ceiling fan whirring unevenly above, bottle-blonde ex-pat butchering 'Bette Davis Eyes' on the karaoke as her Costa crim boyfriend gazed proudly on.

'Drew tells us you've been in Malta.'

Spike looked round. Drew Stanford-Trench's girl had red Pre-Raphaelite hair. As promised, her friend was a brunette. Both had the heavy, hooded eyes that suggested Drew had dragged them into the pub some hours ago.

'We hear it was rather dangerous,' the friend said. She smiled, revealing a smear of pink on her front tooth.

Spike moved his chair to face them. 'Don't listen to anything Drew says. He has a tendency to exaggerate.'

Stanford-Trench was at the bar, taking receipt of a tray of wine glasses and pints.

'I don't mind a bit of danger,' the darker-haired girl added, brushing a hand against Spike's knee.

Stanford-Trench slid the tray onto the table. 'Just had an email which might interest you,' he called over to Spike.

Seeing Spike cup an ear, Stanford-Trench leaned into the red-haired girl and whispered something. The friend broke off her conversation, watching expectantly as Spike stood up.

'What did the email say?' Spike asked once they'd reached a quieter corner of the pub.

'It concerns *The Restless Wave* and its errant crew.'

'Piers Harrington?'

Stanford-Trench shook his head. 'No, Harrington's home-free, lording it up at his flat in Sotogrande. It's to do with the yacht owner, Radovic. Apparently he's a seriously big fish: drugs, prostitution, the lot. A kingpin for the entire Mediterranean region.'

'I thought Radovic was just an alias.'

'One of them. No one knows his real identity, but apparently he has a nickname.'

The girls were beckoning from the table now that the karaoke machine was free.

'She gone,' Stanford-Trench said.

Spike suddenly wheeled round. 'What did you say?'

Stanford-Trench took a step backwards. 'Jesus, Spike. Take it easy. Z-I-G-O-N. It's Serbian or Slovenian or something. *Ži-gon*,' he said in an accent, then waved at the girls. 'OK. Let's get this done.'

He turned and set off towards the stage at the back of the pub. The brunette beckoned to Spike: her smile disappeared as she saw him move for the door, then she downed her glass of wine and consoled herself with the microphone.

6

Coming out into Casemates, Spike saw a group of men in black tie stumbling over the cobbles towards him, yelling out the James Bond theme tune arm in arm. He turned away to the north-west corner of the square. The Rock rose above, pockmarks visible on its flank, tunnel mouths where the inhabitants of Gibraltar – Neanderthals, Greeks, Romans, Moors, Spanish, British – had bored inside for shelter. He thought back to the legend of the Rock's existence that every Gibraltarian schoolchild was taught – a mountain that Hercules had split in two to celebrate one of his labours. Torn apart by a demigod, hacked into by men, yet still standing, proud and immovable.

Spike ducked into an alleyway. Darkness and quiet at last; finally he could think. Head resting against damp concrete, he forced his mind back to the fight with Salib, trying to remember his dying words. She gone. *Žigon* . . .

He checked the time. If he moved quickly, he could be over the Spanish border in half an hour, at Harrington's flat in Sotogrande by 10 p.m. He glanced round, then stopped. A man was backing into the alley, leading a girl by the hand. In the street light gleaming in from the square, Spike made out the profile of the brunette from the pub. A moment later, the couple embraced greedily.

Spike moved towards them through the darkness. As he came closer, he recognised the man's face. He had a hand wedged beneath the girl's top, his sweaty blond curls pressed to her neck. A bow tie was draped over his collar.

'All well, Hamish?' Spike said as he passed. He sensed a commotion behind as he re-entered the square. The Rock rose to the right, silent and steadfast. As Spike turned towards Winston Churchill Avenue, he walked quickly, driven by something which might even have been hope.

A NOTE ON THE AUTHOR

Thomas Mogford has worked as a journalist for *Time Out* and as a translator for the UEFA Champions League. His first novel in the Spike Sanguinetti series, *Shadow of the Rock*, was published by Bloomsbury in 2012; *Sign of the Cross* is his second book. Thomas Mogford is married and lives with his family in London.